# UNLEASHED

*7 Deadly Sins, Greed*

**HALEY RHOADES**

This is a work of fiction. Names, characters, businesses, places, events, and incidents are either the products of the author's imagination or used in a fictitious manner. Any resemblance to actual persons, living or dead, or actual events is purely coincidental.

Any trademarks, service marks, product names, or named features are assumed to be the property of their respective owners and are used only for reference. There is no implied endorsement.

Unleashed, 7 Deadly Sins, Greed
Copyright © 2021 Haley Rhoades
All rights reserved.

Cover Design by Germancreative on Fiverr

Paperback ISBN-10: 1734664669
Paperback ISBN-13: 978-1-7346646-6-9

Want More? Follow Me
www.haleyrhoades.com

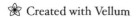 Created with Vellum

# TRIVIA

To Enhance Your Reading of Unleashed
read the Trivia Page near the end of the book
prior to opening chapter #1.

No Spoilers-I promise.

# DEDICATION

*To the first responders that put their lives on the line everyday to keep our communities safe. Thank you for all you sacrifice.*

# PROLOGUE

**Sylvie**

I shoot a quick text to Lidia; she's probably asleep as she has early morning classes tomorrow.

**Me: You will not believe what happened to me**

Immediately, my cell phone rings.

"I thought you'd be asleep," I greet.

"Still studying for a test tomorrow," she explains. "What happened?"

"Well," I begin, "I started painting this afternoon. I got

lost in my canvas. The next thing I know, two police officers were knocking at my door."

"What did they want?" she quickly asks.

"Well, you know the new speakers I had installed today?"

"Yeah..."

"I was listening to my playlist while painting," I share. "I didn't pay attention, and I had the speakers on out by the pool. Anyway, you know how loud I listen to my music. One of my new neighbors called in a noise complaint to the police."

"No way!" Lidia gasps.

"Of course, it just happened to be the time I'm working on an angry portrait, listening to my metal playlist. Let's just say the lyrics were not radio edits." I take a quick breath. "I've made a great first impression on my new neighbors."

"Were the cops nice about it?" Lidia inquires.

"Oh, you should have been here," I giggle. "They sent two very *attractive* cops to my door. One of them was a silver fox and the other a young hottie."

"What?" she sputters. "Seriously, Mom?"

"Yes. The older of the two was tall with silver in his dark hair and his goatee. The younger one was stacked with muscles on top of muscles, dark hair, and dark eyes. I was awestruck as I opened the door. I'm sure I stood there frozen, looking like an idiot in my painting clothes with paint in my hair." Adrenaline still pulsing through me, I try to steady my breath.

"Wow! You're a lucky lady," Lidia chuckles.

"I should have gotten the young hottie's name," I state. "You'd definitely be interested in a date with him."

"Mom, for the last time, stop," she whines. "I don't need you to set me up."

"You say that, but on a scale of one to ten, he was definitely a ten," I share. "The silver fox was a ten, too."

"Mom!" she squeals.

"Okay. Okay," I give in. "Trust me, you would have thought they were hot with a capital H-O-T."

"So, did you get a ticket?" she asks, changing the topic of conversation.

"They let me off with a warning," I share. "I promised I'd be more careful with my outdoor speakers in the future. Get this, though. The young hottie winked and smirked at me when I promised it wouldn't happen again. What does that mean?" I ask. "How should I interpret that?"

"No way," Lidia scoffs. "A cop wouldn't do that. You must have imagined it."

I don't argue with my daughter, but I'm 100 percent sure I didn't imagine it.

## Chapter One
## SYLVIE TWO MONTHS EARLIER

I play with the fresh green leaves of the peony bush sprouting from the ground. "Omar, I can't believe it's been a year already," I begin, sitting myself down at his headstone. "There were times, countless days when I wasn't sure I could take another hour without you. I cursed the mornings I woke up and the nights without you by my side." I pause, calling up all my strength to do this. Like the leaves on this bush, although I am the same person, I change daily.

"I've mourned your absence *every* single day." I fight back the tears stinging my sinuses, threatening to escape the cages of my lids. "With the help of Lidia and my therapist, Edith, somehow, I made it through." I look up to the bright blue sky. The clouds float effortlessly across like all is well in the world.

"I need to apologize to you." I trace the engraved letters of his name as I speak. "I got lost in our lives. I changed everything about myself and no longer resembled the girl you fell in love with. For that, I am sorry." I sigh deeply. "I got caught up in what the wife and life of a law firm partner should be and lost sight of who I was. How you stayed with me all those years without mentioning it... I'll never know." I release a hollow chuckle. "Don't get me wrong; we had a great life. You worked hard to provide every opportunity for our daughter, and you bought me a beautiful home."

"I hope you know how much Lidia and I love you and miss you. Even if it looks as if we're moving on, we struggle with your absence." I sigh, gathering my emotions and finding the words I need to share.

"I have a meeting at the firm tomorrow; they claim to have settled the estate. It will be my first time there since you passed. My therapist claims it's another bit of closure that I need." I shake my head. "I don't think I can go back there. The memories of you in every inch of that office make it hard. Walking through the parking lot where I last saw you will be... difficult."

The image of Omar lying on the cold concrete, a white sheet covering him as the police and EMTs hovered nearby, burns in my memory. I bounce back and forth on whether I wish I had not been the one to find him that night or not. Most often, I'm glad I found him rather than having officers delivering the news on my doorstep. However, the last image of him that comes to mind isn't at his funeral, serene in his casket. I see him lying on the ground alone in the darkness.

I'm startle when my cell phone pings.

"That's my cue," I state, returning my eyes to his name. "It's time to meet Lidia for dinner." I stand, dusting off the grass and dirt from my pants. "We're okay, more so day after day. I love you." I kiss my fingers and press them over the letters engraved on the stone, the same ones forever written on my heart.

## Chapter Two
# SYLVIE

Late in the week, I patiently wait on the sofa as Edith places her glasses over her nose and opens her tablet to take notes.

"So, how are you today, Sylvie?"

Her question has many answers, answers that she will pry, dig, and pillage for until I open up and let her in. I've decided not to mention the estate meeting at Omar's firm early next week. I can't discuss my feelings on returning to the office. They're too raw, and I don't think I could endure an hour on the topic.

"I'm pretty good," I state honestly.

"In our last session, we discussed the approaching anniversary of Omar's passing." She spins her stylus in her left hand as she speaks to me. "Tell me about that."

"Well, I went to visit his grave," I share. "I bet I spent an hour there, talking to him. I did that early in the morning then spent the rest of the day in Iowa City with Lidia."

"What did you talk to Omar about?"

*There's the digging she's so good at.* "Well, I told him how much I miss him—*we* miss him," I correct. "And I told him it's hard, but Lidia and I are doing okay."

"How did you feel then you left the cemetery?"

*There she goes again with the questioning.* "It felt good," I confess. "Like a heavy load lifted. I know that's not polite to say…"

"Isn't it?" Edith cuts me off. "Isn't being honest, taking ownership of your mourning, and saying the words out loud, okay?"

*She's like a spider on a web; she maneuvers our conversations from one strand to another then explains how they all intersect.*

"I might not admit it to everyone, but yes. The work we've done really helps," I state.

"It's the work you've done," she corrects. "I've only guided you on the path; the work has been all yours. Will you continue to visit his grave monthly?" she inquires, typing on her tablet.

"I'm not sure. I think I will visit when I want to but not write it on a calendar as a weekly commitment." I shrug, looking down at my hands folded in my lap. "I've felt I owed it to him and Lidia to visit this past year, but I don't feel that way anymore. I'm ready to focus more on myself."

She nods, adding additional text to her notes. "So, the goal was socializing this week. How did that go?" Edith asks from her overstuffed plaid chair, facing me.

I reposition myself on the small sofa with a pillow tight to my chest. I keep my eyes on the table between us. "I stayed after church for a cup of coffee and cookies." I uncross my legs, letting them remain apart. "I spoke to a few families."

"Good." Edith is always positive. "How did you feel?"

I shrug.

"Any upcoming church events to attend? Any potential friends?" she prompts.

I shake my head. "And I didn't look into any book clubs or card clubs."

"Why?" she asks, always trying to uncover true reasons for my actions—or lack thereof. "Why are you hesitating to socialize?"

Again, I shrug. "I feel like the new girl in a large school. No one approaches me, and I'm hesitant to engage."

Edith taps her stylus on the tablet in her lap. "Would you like to set this as a goal again?"

When I nod, she continues, "Let's look at the local library and bookstore for book clubs." Edith suggests this as if she'll go with me. "Facebook groups and community calendars might be a good place to look, too."

I nod. I understand that I need to find hobbies and make friends. I've avoided these in the past, devoting all of my time and talents to Lidia and our family.

Once again, Edith looks at her notes from our previous session. "Did you bring your notebook with your lists?" she inquires.

I pull the spiral notebook from my purse, turning several pages to the lists we made in sessions this year.

"As you read through the lists, how do you feel?" she asks.

My mind rewinds to the past session in which we started a running list of items that I wished to revisit on the anniversary of Omar's death. As I mourned during our appointments, I also took a long hard look at myself. We discussed the woman I am compared to the woman I want to be.

When I met and dated Omar, I envisioned becoming a woman and having a life very different from the one I became and lived.

"I think I'm both excited and scared," I admit.

"What excites you?" She prompts more discussion.

"Each item," I answer. "I can't wait to start."

"What scares you?" She digs deeper.

"I worry about what Lidia might think of my new tasks and hobbies." I shrug, lifting my eyes from the lists to my therapist.

"Why would Lidia's reactions bother you?"

"Her father's death was hard on her. She seems fine on campus as her life there remains the same as it was over a year ago." I move the pillow from my lap back to the corner of the sofa, placing my open notebook on the cushion beside me. "When she returns to Des Moines, though, the fact that Omar isn't here becomes a reality. I think moving to a new house will help her as all of his memories are in the home the three of us shared."

I take a sip of water to quench my dry mouth, then continue, "I worry that my new tasks and hobbies will be yet another change that upsets her."

"What have we discussed about how others feel about your life?"

*Yeah, yeah. I know.* "I need to live the life I want, doing the things of interest to me, and I shouldn't let others prevent me from my happiness. I need to put myself first." I repeat the answer we've covered in every session of the past year.

"That is one of the items on your 'reminder list,'" she tells me.

I turn to another page. On it, in large handwriting, are

the words, "Live the life I want. Don't let others prevent me."

"I'd like for you to share your lists with Lidia as well as all the feelings we've discussed," Edith encourages, not for the first time. "She might enjoy helping you place check marks by items on your list."

*She's right; I know Lidia supports me and wants me to be happy.* It came up when she admitted she knew of my painting hobby. I thought I'd kept hidden for years.

"Which one do you hope to try first?" Edith continues, directing the session.

"I'd like to learn to use more technology and start practicing the guitar," I share. "I plan to schedule an appointment at the Apple store. I hear they are the best at teaching you how to use devices and fix them if there is an issue." I look at her. "And I'm playing around with the idea of applying to be a part-time piano teacher at the music store. That's where I will take my guitar lessons, too."

Edith alternates between taking notes and looking at me as I speak.

"I've tried to research using the internet on my phone, but it's so old that it takes forever and is too small to read on. So, I think the Apple store will be my first task."

"Sounds good," Edith praises. "Before our next session, you will plan to look into groups at church or book clubs at the bookstore and visit the Apple store."

"Yep," I agree, closing my notebook.

Excitement defeats the fear within me. My blood hums through my body. *I'm ready.* Today, I'm ready to start on my lists.

## Chapter Three
# SYLVIE

*I hate Mondays.* My stomach roils as I enter the law firm—Omar's practice. I haven't been here in the year since Omar passed. I tried to prepare myself, knowing everything would remind me of him, but obviously, I failed. The air feels heavy and hot. It hurts my chest to breathe. I keep my eyes focused on the carpet before me and the artwork on the wall opposite me for fear I might lose what little hold I have on my emotions.

The receptionist cuts my misery short, taking me to the conference room. Sitting at the long table, I feel like I took a punch in the gut. Just like his office at home, this was Omar's world. I can't help but remember him in this setting.

I take the long breaths Edith taught me. Then, rather than panic, I name objects across from me. *Leather chair, painting, intercom...* I say to myself.

"Sylvie, so nice to see you again." The partners take turns greeting me then take seats opposite me. The three men open binders in front of them on the table. I realize all three attend this meeting out of respect for their former partner and to comfort me, but I'd rather speak to one lawyer and hurry through this. I want this finished once and for all.

"Will Lidia be joining us today?" One partner politely asks.

I shake my head.

"Right, so as we've previously mentioned, Omar wisely invested his money over the years..."

I do my best to listen to their words, but my mind flashes between them and memories of Omar.

"Life insurance... Trust fund... Stocks and bonds... House... Van... Car..."

I hear words, but I'm not listening. They place a large binder in front of me. I stare at page after page of its figures and words; it's all too much. I'll need to read it at home when I can focus.

The hour-long meeting passes in a blur. I shake all of their hands and promise to seek their assistance if Lidia or I ever need anything. Still in a trance, somehow, I drive myself safely to the house. I place the binder on the counter and pour a large glass of red wine.

---

I open the financial binder, passing the title page and firm's contact information quickly. In front of me, I see figures, figures that blow my mind.

During our marriage, Omar allowed me $3,000 monthly in my account for household expenses, Lidia's needs, and incidentals. I paid utilities, groceries, and gas from that allowance.

I pinched pennies for years, making do with what he allowed. I clipped coupons, shopped deals, and did without many things I longed to do or own. From my measly monthly allowance, I saved $7,500 over the years. It pales in comparison to Omar's savings.

I knew my name was on the house and minivan. I had no clue there were these other assets. Listed as his sole beneficiary, I now possess much more than my meager savings account.

A trust fund of over $450,000 is in Lidia's name and available upon settling his estate. I'm not surprised that Omar took care of us in case of his passing. It's the amount of money that shocks me to my core. I'm not sure how Lidia will react when I share this news with her.

The house, minivan, and his car are all paid for. The firm secured copies of Omar's death certificate and updated titles for each with my name on them. We bought our house over 20 years ago for $275,000. An enclosed appraisal shows its value is now over $400,000.

Omar's other accounts and investments total over $3.6 million, and this does not include his million-dollar life insurance policy.

I take deep breaths and name things I see around the room as I hope to prevent a panic attack. *Light bulb, house plant, chair, centerpiece...*

I scrimped to save and worried about money every day of our marriage. I did my best to make do with my allowance while he provided a comfortable life for us. Omar knew of these assets and never shared that information with me. *How naïve I have been, how stupid.*

I should have been more involved with taxes and finances; I should have asked questions. Instead, I allowed Omar to take care of me and our daughter; I should have taken an active role in our savings.

Nauseous, I pull crackers from the pantry to calm my stomach as my head pounds. Figures swarm in my mind; it's too much money. I'm not sure what to do. The partners referred me to a financial management firm to assist me. My head swims.

I sip the last drops from my wine glass and pour myself another. A deep breath—in and out, in and out—calms me.

In therapy, I discussed selling the house, downsizing, and using some proceeds for items on my list. This is to be my year to "find me," and I thought a little money would help me do that. With this much money, I can do anything I choose. The enormity of the events and hobbies on my list pales compared to the lists of investments Omar compiled during our time together.

*Why did I hide my head in the sand for so many years?*

## Chapter Four
## SYLVIE

After such a long day, I should be asleep, but I can't lie another minute in this bed. I slip out from under the covers. My slightly ajar closet door catches my eye. I grab both knobs in my hands, flinging the doors wide open.

I cringe at the plethora of pantsuits in muted colors before me. I've always craved vibrant, trendier styles but sacrificed my desires for the "proper attire" a wife of a lawyer would wear. I wrap my fingers around the hanger of a beige jacket and matching pants. I lift it from the closet and place it over the end of the bed to donate. *I'm definitely donating these.* Pantsuits in pale blue, navy, cream, and black, one after another, I purge from my closet. I snag a couple of hangers at a time and move them to the growing pile on the end of my bed.

Staring at the pile, I recall overhearing a conversation at a Bible study that one charity in town collects attire for women to wear for job interviews. They collect donations and help the women practice for the interviews, setting them up for success by giving them a hand up, not a handout. *Teaching women in need the art of successful interviews is a charity I can get behind.*

Back at the closet, I squeeze five hangers between my hands then toss the pantsuits into the donation pile. Armful after armful of pantsuits vacate my closet, creating a giant pile at the end of the bed. Amidst the pant suits are silk blouses, sweaters, and silk scarves.

*Free.* I finally feel free of these shackles. They were costumes I endured to play my role of doting wife. My love for Omar prevented me from straying from the neutral colors and styles. Now, I can dress as I please. There's nothing holding me back.

The rod empty, except for two button down blouses and a pair of black slacks, I turn my attention to the shoe boxes on the shelf above. I pull them down two at a time and pile them next to my other donations. I need not read the labels. Inside are granny shoes in muted tones. Sensible, one-inch, square-heeled shoes to match each of my pantsuits.

I refuse to wear them again. I'm ready to own blue jeans, t-shirts, and other items in vibrant hues. I plan to purchase clothes that reflect my personality.

There's an empty closet before me. Excitement grows for me meeting with a personal shopper. I'm done with the boxy, old lady clothes and eager to start on my new wardrobe to express the true me.

*Chapter Five*

# SYLVIE

"Mom!" Lidia calls from the kitchen.

I love the weekends she comes home from college. This house is too big and quiet for one person.

"Hmm?" I mumble, while watering my snake plant in the front room.

"It's still not up here," my daughter states in a maternal tone, hands propped on her hips.

"You're gonna make me regret telling you about my therapy sessions and assignments," I inform her as I make my way to the kitchen. I stand opposite her at the island, my forearms leaning on the granite countertop.

"The reason you started sharing in the first place was to hold yourself accountable." Lidia poses, hands remaining on her hips and a scowl upon her face.

"Fine," I huff in defeat. I point to the drawer by the refrigerator. "It's in there."

She doesn't ask for permission. Instead, she opens the drawer and places my list on the center of the fridge door, securing it with two magnets. She takes one step back then another, tilting her head to the side as she reads.

Mentally, I go over the handwritten list on notebook paper as she does.

**The list:**
**Learn to use technology**
**Paint more**
**Share my art**
**Learn to play guitar**
**Explore restaurants**
**Discover me, inside and out**
**Participate in the world outside of my house**
**Make friends and find a best friend**
**Ride a motorcycle**
**Get a dog**
**Attend concerts**
**Take a road trip**
**Sky dive, bungee jump, hot-air balloon ride**
**Travel to: New Orleans, Nashville, Washington D.C., Tampa, Denver, Dallas**
**Get a passport**
**Travel to: Mexico, Aruba, the Caribbean, Greece, Egypt**

My heart rate quickens as she reads it; I've only shared it

with Edith. In the past year, I've come to realize there is a lot about me my daughter doesn't know as I've kept it hidden. I plan to ease her into it one at a time, but my list might cause her to have many questions.

Lidia turns to face me, a giant grin upon her face. It's his grin and his eyes; Lidia looks so much like her father. My heart melts.

"Let me hear it," I challenge, eager to move past this awkward conversation.

She shakes her head, smile growing larger. "I like it."

*She likes it? What on Earth does that mean? She likes it? Does she think it's a farce?* The mother she knows doesn't do the items on that list.

Lidia chews on her lower lip for a moment. "I've long known you've hidden your talents. I found the key to your craft room when I was 12." She pauses for my reaction.

I nod. I knew she'd known about the painting for a while.

"Grandma and Dad shared stories of how the two of you met and what you were like." Lidia pulls a water bottle from the fridge. "Dad's face lit up when he spoke of meeting you and the dates he took you on."

I never knew. She loved her daddy-daughter time; I had no idea they spoke of such things. *When he shared with her, did he miss that part of me? Did he long for the woman he fell in love with, and if so, why didn't he tell me?*

"I can't wait to see you take time for these things that interest you. I'm here if you need me for anything: for a ride, a pep talk, advice, or to practice on. I know you need to do it on your own, but I'm ready to help when needed." She laughs. "And I'm willing to be your plus one as you travel."

Her wide smile touches her twinkling eyes. I marvel at her excitement as I approach and pull her into a tight hug.

Holding my shoulders with both hands, arms extended, she states, "Some of these are pretty dangerous feats and lofty goals."

## Chapter Six
# SYLVIE

As each week passes, I grow stronger and stronger. It's time, time for me to pack everything up to keep, donate, or sell. I've encouraged Lidia to box up the items important to her over her last three visits. With those items out of the house, it's time to thin out, move out, and put the house up for sale.

Following the suggestions of the staging company, I take all family photos down, clear off all surfaces, and plan to clear as much furniture from the house as possible before they stage it to sell.

The clothes I plan to donate to charity. I spoke to my minister and his wife; as I sell everything, I plan to donate all proceeds to the ministries of the church if they assist me. We've decided to hold an indoor rummage sale of sorts at my open house to announce the house is for sale and hopefully get rid of the furniture the same day. Most of the furniture is over 10 years old, but it's still in excellent condition. We're hoping the sale saves us from moving the furniture multiple times; and after it's gone, the staging company can get the house ready for showings.

I recall during Lidia's first year of college telling Omar this house was too big. It feels even more so in the year since his death. It's time for a simpler home with new furniture. Although I love this house, I need a new one, one where memories of my old life won't haunt the new me rising to the surface.

Ready to address Omar's memory haunting me, I sit ready to reply to an uncomfortable email I received yesterday. My fingers flex while I search for a plan. I stare at the email. Clicking reply, I fidget in my seat. Honest. I'll just be honest.

I don't want to see it; I don't want to know what might have taken place in his work apartment. It was Omar's secret, and I don't want to know. I'd rather live with my memories of his occasional sleeping at the office during big trials. In my memory he worked until the wee hours of the morning, cleaning himself up in the bathroom before he returned to court.

"Please donate all items from the apartment, including the funds from the sale of the property. Use the funds to do pro bono work at the firm. Sincerely, Sylvic Rice"

I click send, breathing a sigh of relief that Omar's law partners will take care of the matter. It's no longer my problem.

## Chapter Seven
## SYLVIE

Boxing again today, I'm in the kitchen, I snag another box. *Three! It's crazy; who needs three boxes of cookbooks?* In my constant search for recipes to impress Omar, I gathered an entire library of cookbooks.

The irony, more often than not, is that my culinary endeavors lay on chilled plates in the refrigerator until Omar called it quits at the office. Although he called to alert me, he would work late. The call came as dinner was already baking. With his limited time at home, I found food was a way to receive praise from him and impress colleagues when hosting a dinner party.

*I won't need these cookbooks.* Cooking for one isn't easy, but very few recipes serve only one; I don't need leftovers.

After dinner, I'm not making much progress on packing up

the photo albums. In my nostalgia, I take my time, flipping through each one. In years past, with free time on my hands, I took my time in creating each album page.

Pregnant with Lidia, I look so young. I smile, realizing I was younger than Lidia is now. In the photos of Omar holding Lidia, it's easy to see his love for our daughter. With each photo, a moment of time replays in my head. Here she toddled in her playroom; here she attempted to climb the stairs for the first time.

In the next album are Lidia's birthdays, two pages for each year. In the early years, Omar's parents and my mom were the only guests. When she started school, classmates began attending the parties.

Another album holds photos of Lidia at the piano, practicing and at recitals. These photos are bittersweet now that I have learned how much she hated playing. It wasn't until the past year that she confessed her distaste.

The only constant in the scrapbooks, with all of their photos, is my hair. I don't know when I decided to keep the style, requiring little maintenance and no coloring, for decades.

*It's time I choose a new hairstyle.*

---

Later, with all my linens in boxes, I notice two smaller boxes on the highest shelf of the closet. Not remembering the contents, I pull both down to the floor before peeking inside. *Whoa.* These are boxes holding my journals; these notebooks contain my thoughts and desires from age 18 until Lidia's sophomore year of high school.

I flip through a notebook, marveling at the handwriting filling each page and often the margins. I pause, reading the entries. One topic I ranted about was a concert nearby, one that I longed to attend, and how inappropriate it was for Omar's wife. Another topic included locations I hoped someday to visit. Sadly, I didn't attend the concert or travel to any of the places I wrote about.

In another notebook, I find a bucket list I created at age 18. Little did I know then the complete 180-degree turn my life would take in the next three years.

I look at my accomplishments over the past 21 years. I nurtured and taught Lidia to become a woman confident in her strengths, owning the fortitude to survive in the modern times. I guess, learning from my mistakes, I raised her not to give up on her dreams; I taught her that she can have it all—a family and a career.

While I raised our daughter, I helped Omar earn a partnership by mingling at dinner parties and social functions, all the while keeping his confidence high, even during the tough cases.

Omar and Lidia's accomplishments might be seen as mine; I don't see it that way. I'm a wonderful mother and was a great wife; those are my two accomplishments. Somehow, they don't seem enough in my own eyes.

I long to find this younger version of me, the woman full of confidence and hope, the woman that does what she wants instead of worrying how it might look to others. This is the woman I've discussed with Edith and plan to find again.

## Chapter Eight
# SYLVIE

The next day, I'm giddy; in this store with all of its possibilities, I feel like a kid in the candy shop. I've wiggled every mouse then touched every iPad and iPhone on display. My breath catches when a woman greets, "Welcome to the Apple Store. What can I help you with today?"

"I'm moving into the new century as my daughter says," I state. "I'm interested in an iPhone." I show her my now antiquated cell phone. "And perhaps an iPad, Apple TV, and laptop."

"Okay. Let's start with your phone..." Her face lights up with the dollars I plan to spend today.

Over two hours later, I'm driving home with all four items, accessories, and future appointments to attend classes in the store to learn how to use each of my products. I've so much to learn about using these technologies. Lidia gave me a sneak peek; now, I'm curious to learn it all.

The next day, with three pictures of me, ages 18 to 20, I walk into the department store, excited. In the past, I've dreaded shopping. Now, I know that was because I wasn't purchasing the items I craved. *Why did I give up on my taste in fashion so easily?*

I approach the customer service area, our agreed upon meeting place, and am immediately approached by the personal shopper. When she asks what I'm looking for, I give her more than she expects. I hand her the photos, claiming I want to return to the styles I wore all those years ago.

When Lidia asked why I wanted a personal shopper, I shared that while I know what I like, I don't know where to look and how to accessorize according to current trends. The shopper could help me spot items.

When discussing it at my last session with Edith, I explained I wanted to "find me."

To which she asked, "Have you been lost?"

We discussed how I was not lost, just playing a role for years. I still admired styles and trends I like from a distance as they didn't fit the professional agenda. In my journals, my true thoughts and desires for clothes were expressed. They were just hidden away; it's time they surface.

I share with the personal shopper that I don't have formal functions or work to dress up for. I'm interested in casual styles that are expressions of me and would like to start with a few outfits today. Together, we choose jeans, many brightly colored shirts, retro tees, and comfy sweats. Although she works for the department store, she mentions I might find concert shirts and other t-shirts I desire at thrift stores or consignment shops. I make a note to check them out in the weeks to come.

As I drive from the mall to my house, I glance at the multitude of shopping bags in the back seat. I didn't just buy a couple of outfits. My new wardrobe is well on its way. I have two pairs of Converse shoes, two pairs of boots, and a sassy pair of sandals. I also have not one but four pairs of jeans along with some shorts for summer. A couple of swimsuits and a denim jacket complete my purchases.

Next to the white bags from the department store, the pink bags from Victoria's Secret pop brightly. I return my eyes to the highway before me, proud I splurged on the pretty bra and panties sets.

Once home, I spend the rest of the afternoon shopping online. I order handbags, belts, a designer blazer, and two sundresses.

With the help of the shopper, I now know what I want and clammer to buy them. I spend over an hour on Amazon after I've visited several major clothing stores' websites.

Edith's words play in my mind. "Remember baby steps; it's a process. You *will* make mistakes. Think of them as learning opportunities."

I didn't take baby steps today. I plunged into shopping for my wardrobe headfirst.

---

Continuing my transformation, today I'm addressing my outdated hairstyle. I've been excited to find something new that expresses the woman I'm trying to find. In bed, I meticulously browse celebrity sites and Pinterest, critiquing hairstyles and colors. Excited about the short, sassy style I like, I need to find a salon; I no longer want to pop into the no-appointment-needed shop in the strip mall.

During the next week, with the assistance of my new devices, I visit Yelp and Facebook to read reviews on nearby salons. Finding the one for me, I call an Aveda salon with all natural products nearby.

## Chapter Nine
# SYLVIE

Today is the day; today, I morph my hairstyle to match my personality. I approach the salon chair, excited to embrace this change.

"What are we doing today?" my new stylist asks while draping a black cape around me, securing it with Velcro behind my neck.

I pull my arm with my cell phone in hand from beneath the cape and pull up the screenshots I saved. "I like this style," I state. "Will it work with my face shape?"

The stylist takes my phone, swipes through the photos, then looks closely at my face in the mirror. She pulls my hair away from my face and off my neck in the back, still scrutinizing my reflection.

"Yes, if you are ready to make the drastic change, it will work well with your cheekbones."

I breathe a tiny sigh of relief. I had my heart set on this style; I'm not sure what I'd choose if she hadn't agreed.

"The style is versatile," she shares. "You can curl it, scrunch it, or simply blow it dry. You mentioned color when you scheduled your appointment. What were you thinking?"

I shrug. "This is where I'd like your input. I've never colored my hair. I'm ready to; I'm just not sure what I need."

She runs her fingers through sections of my hair along my part and near my face.

"I don't see many grays, so we can do one color all over or add highlights." She still plays with small sections of my hair. "All over color requires you to come in regularly as the roots will show when they grow out. Highlights and lowlights are more natural and blend better as they grow out. Should you decide to keep the new, shorter style, you'll be in often for a trim, and we can touch up both as needed."

I nod in the mirror. "Let's add natural highlights for the summer," I decide, and she smiles her approval.

Moments later, she chops inches off the side of my hair. "So, are you new to town?"

---

That night, while I wait in the tiny room for my guitar teacher to start my second lesson, I practice my fingering over the frets.

"What new song did you learn this week?" my teacher asks, entering the room.

I shrug, too embarrassed to share.

"C'mon," he encourages. "You told me you pretty much watch a video and then play the song. So, let me have it. What song?"

"*Hotel California*," I answer. "And *American Pie*."

He smiles, slowly shaking his head. "Only two?" he teases.

"And part of *Redemption Song*," I confess.

"Let me hear," he prompts.

As I play the two songs I've practiced every day this week, my heart warms; music seems to soothe my soul.

"I'm wasting your time with lessons," he states. "You are a talented woman. Your ear for music is far superior to any I've ever encountered." He passes me his business card. "I've written my cell number on the back. If there ever comes a time that you have a question on a technique or song, feel free to call me."

Carrying my guitar case, I wave goodbye to the staff as I make my way to the car. I enjoy playing guitar and challenging myself to conquer a new song. I'll let the internet be my teacher from now on.

During my drive, I contemplate songs I might like to play. Although I love the simplistic sounds of the acoustic guitar, many songs of interest to me include electric guitars.

*Hmm. I might need to buy one.*

---

Early Monday, I'm reading the local news on my iPad, enjoying a cup of coffee, when my cell phone signals a text.

**Lidia: Are you free today?**
**Me: Yes**
**Lidia: I'm driving to Des Moines after class**
**Lidia: Spend afternoon together & dinner**

**Me: Yay!**
**Lidia: I'll text when on my way**


I'd planned to paint all day; Lidia's visit is a better plan.

## Chapter Ten
# SYLVIE

"Did you buy out the Apple Store?" Lidia teases, marveling at my new devices on the kitchen island when she arrives. "I'm jealous."

"Please," I scoff. "You've had a smartphone and a laptop all of your life."

"Do you know how to use them?" she asks, pulling water from the fridge.

"I've attended three classes at the Apple Store," I remind her. "I know the basics and plan to take more classes as I grow more familiar with each."

"Grab your phone," she directs, pulling hers from her back pocket. "Let's download Snapchat and sign you up."

She walks me step by step through downloading the app then creating an account. My head spins a bit as she shows me all the filters, stickers, and camera angles to use within the app.

"I use Snapchat more than texts," she states. "Let's send

your first Snap. What would you like to take a pic of?"

I point to my guitar on the sofa in the front room. With her help, I take a picture, type a short label, add a sticker, then send it to her. She shows me the Snap on her phone.

"Snapchat is easier than sending a photo via text. Here. Let me move the app to the front screen of your phone."

I watch her fingers fly on the screen in hopes that I may be able to repeat the task in the future.

"There. All set." She smiles proudly. Pointing to the sofa, she asks, "How are your guitar lessons going?"

"It's only been a month," I remind her. "I've stopped taking private lessons and use YouTube now."

Lidia shakes her head. "I'm jealous. I wish I could watch a video or hear a song and mimic it. Unlike you, it takes me months to learn a piece of music."

"Not this again," I sigh. "I thought you enjoyed the piano lessons. If you'd told me how you felt, I'd have ended them before you turned 13."

"I'm over it now," she vows. "If I had your ear and talent, I'd probably still be playing. Who knows? I might have even joined a band."

We chuckle together. Like her father, Lidia is driven by numbers. When she left for college, I worried she chose her major to impress him. However, as she talks about her classes, her excitement is evident. Along with her looks, it's another way she reminds me of Omar.

"Play me something," she challenges.

Other than my former teacher, she's my first audience. As I position the acoustic guitar in my lap, I take a few deep breaths and flex my fingers.

I let my hands caress the strings as I play The Black

Crowes' song *She Talks to Angels*. I focus on my fingers and the notes then lose myself in the song.

When it ends, I slowly raise my eyes to Lidia who still stands in the center of the room. Her mouth forms a small "O" and tears fill her eyes. She fans her face, unable to speak.

Knowing she needs a moment, I play *Patience* by Guns N' Roses. It's a long song, so when she sits beside me, I end in the middle of it.

"So jealous," Lidia laughs. "Is there anything you can't play?"

"I'm learning a couple of new songs each week," I share. "The songs I'm working on now are not acoustic."

"So..." Lidia draws. "You need to buy an electric guitar."

"Um..." I purse my lips to the side. "I've already bought one. It's in the corner." I point across the room.

She hops from the sofa. "Oh my, Mom! This is not just an electric guitar." She looks back to me as she points to it. "I follow enough music and pop culture to know a Les Paul is a big deal. How much did this cost you?"

I shake my head, not willing to share the price. *I enjoy playing the guitar and never plan to stop; I splurged on myself, and it feels good.*

## Chapter Eleven
# SYLVIE

After driving through the dealership lots for the twentieth time over the weekend, today, I'm ready to purchase a new vehicle. I park my minivan near the building then make my way to the red Honda Pilot parked in the front row of the vehicle lot. I cup my hands at the sides of my face and put them against the glass to peer inside. I move from window to window, repeating the process.

I don't need my minivan as I won't be transporting Lidia and her friends every day. I want versatility to carry my new canvases but still hold four people comfortably if needed. It's another change for my new life.

Next, I look at the Pilots on either side of the red one. These both have cloth seats, and I prefer the leather. As I walk from vehicle to vehicle, I catch a salesman watching me from the corner of my eye. I'm sure he's hovering, waiting to jump in for the sale. I walk back to the red vehicle.

"How are you this morning?" a male voice calls to me.

I turn to find the salesman in a grey, pin-striped suit approaching. He's balding on top, and he attempts to hide it by spiking his longer hair on each side upward.

"Nice choice. Very safe," he states, mere feet from me. "What exactly are you looking for?"

I point toward the building where I parked. "I'm ready to trade in my minivan, and I think this is what I want. May I take a test drive?"

"Will your husband be joining us?" he inquires, his eyes searching the lot.

"No," I state, trying to hold back my anger. His question insinuates I need a man to make such a purchase.

"Yep. Let me go grab the keys." He smiles, shakes his head, then turns and walks away. "Oh..." He stops, glancing over his shoulder at me. "Um, would it be possible for me to get your keys to have the guys look over the minivan, assess its trade-in value?"

I squint at him as I try to work through it in my mind. *Is this something they always do? I thought that Kelley Blue Book thing was how they determined my van's value.* I've looked it up online and know exactly how much I will want for the trade-in.

"Okay," I answer, searching my purse for the keys.

---

I park the Pilot where I found it. Now, I'm certain this is my new vehicle. I'm in love, but I try to hide that fact from the salesman so he doesn't think he has the upper hand.

"When could your husband come by for a test drive?" he asks as we exit the vehicle.

"He doesn't need to know," I reply.

The salesman's face scrunches, not happy with my answer; he thinks he's lost the sale.

"We can discuss the trade-in value of your minivan," he suggests, motioning to the showroom. "Then, you can take the information home to discuss." He remains tight at my side as we walk. It's almost like he's glued himself to me so I can't escape.

"Have a seat," he directs in his cubicle. He begins looking through the envelope from my glove box that someone used my keys to get for him.

"I'm ready to sign paperwork right now," I blurt, catching him off guard.

"Well, we can't do paperwork until your spouse comes in. Since he is on the title to the minivan, he will have to be present to sign the paperwork."

*Is he's man-splaining this to me?*

I pull Omar's death certificate and the replacement title from my purse and slide it across the wooden desktop. "I'm a widow." I try to hide my contempt for his assumptions.

"Oh... Sorry..." he sputters while I'm sure his mind is working on a new game plan to close the sale.

I use his guilt to knock $5,000 off the price of the Pilot and get every dollar Kelley Blue Book stated my minivan is worth. Driving home, I giggle at his expression when I paid cash. I'm used to assumptions that I need a man to care for me; I love that I am now able to prove them wrong.

## Chapter Twelve
# SYLVIE

The silence in the house makes it hard for me to fall asleep. Only on the second story, it feels as if I'm high in a skyscraper. Every noise I make echoes louder as I box up room by room.

I turn on the lamp, prop my back against the headboard, and bring my iPad to life. I need to find a new place; I'm ready to leave this much-too-large, two-story home and the memories it constantly replays. Lots of happy times in Lidia's childhood cause me to smile while Omar's empty office and side of the bed haunt me. I long for a place to make new memories.

With the assistance of the search engine, I enter my desired filters, and a large list of properties fills the screen. Though Lidia claims I don't need to have a room for her, I still plan for her bedroom and a guest room. The homes span all the cities that make up greater Des Moines. Moving from Norwalk into the city will cut my drive times by several minutes as I make new friends and engage in new hobbies.

When I created my list of pros and cons of moving with all the features I desire, I needed a studio with plenty of light to paint in, a room for Lidia, and one for guests. Of the four-bedroom homes, I rule out the brick ones. I like stonework but not the red brick exterior.

I'm partial to open floor plans and ranch homes. I prefer the laundry to be on the same level as the kitchen and master bedroom, because although they aren't a problem now, in the future, as I age, stairs may be an issue for me.

As I scroll through the list, clicking on picture after picture, I also consider the location. I want easy access to the major roads in the city. If my goal, as discussed with Edith, is to socialize, I'll drive around more.

I hover my index finger over a blonde-stone covered ranch near the Easter Lake portion of south Des Moines with a large, paved surface attached to the three-car garage and a tiny, well-manicured front lawn. It's less for me to mow, so I tap on it and swipe through the pics. It has only three bedrooms.

*Oh, what's this? A beautiful four-season room. That would make a great studio and an in-ground swimming pool. Hmm...*

Excitement pulses through me as I send the property to my real estate agent and then to Lidia.

Seconds later, I jump at my vibrating cell phone.

**Lidia: Why aren't you asleep?**
**Me: Why aren't you?**
**Lidia: Flipping through pics now**

**Me: It has everything I want & then some**
**Lidia: (heart emoji) Pool**
**Lidia: I call the 2nd master when not at school**
**Me: (heart emoji)**
**Me: That's what I wanted to hear**
**Lidia: Need to go study**
**Lidia: Keep me posted**
**Me: Study hard, I (heart emoji) you**

Our conversation over, I scan through the texts one more time. I'm proud I used the emojis like she showed me a couple of days ago. I chuckle, remembering her overly dramatic proclamation about her ushering me into the new century.

## Chapter Thirteen
# SYLVIE

Three weeks later, with piles of paperwork complete, I grab a quick lunch then hurry to my new house. I've scheduled electricians today and find they're waiting in front of the house when I pull in.

"I'm sorry," I greet as they exit their van.

"No worries," the driver says. "We're running ahead of schedule."

The team of two men and one woman follows me into the house. I show them around, and we discuss the location of the speakers throughout the house: upstairs and down and on the patio around the pool. They promise to install some disguised as landscaping rocks on the patio near the pool. I motion to the walls I want the flat screens mounted on in the living room, family room, master bedrooms, and guest bedroom.

The female instructs the two men which tasks to start on. I guess she's in charge. *Right on-girl power.*

Three hours to install and a 15-minute tour, then I receive instructions on the command center in the kitchen. They leave a thick booklet on the counter by the console; it's a bit daunting with all the buttons and knobs. Before they leave, they assist me with starting my playlist, then my music blasts throughout the house.

I slowly spin, taking in the open floor plan of the ground floor. Once the furniture arrives, it will feel like home; it's my new home in which to create fresh memories and start my new life, the new life 19-year-old me imagined all those years ago: artful, bright, expressive, and riddled with adventures.

After inflating the air mattress in the living room, it takes three trips to carry my easel and paint supplies in from the garage. The mattress and easel are the only furniture in the large, empty space that comprises my living room, kitchen, dining room, and attached sunroom.

I quickly send a picture of the new space to Lidia on Snapchat, highlighting the air mattress and the fact that tonight is my first night in the new house.

I still have possession of the old house, but I'm excited to start this new part of my life. I figure I'm not going to sleep tonight in either location; standing in the large empty space, I'm glad I brought my paint supplies to keep me busy.

I set up the easel in the sunroom—my new studio—spread out my paints, drop a canvas tarp on the floor, and fan out my brushes. As Seether plays through the speakers, I open my duffle on the floor to pull out my overalls and head into the bathroom to change. My skin prickles as the excitement of an empty canvas upon my easel and millions of colors at my disposal to bend to my will fills me.

I mix colors on the palette in my left hand before I brush dark strokes, shadows, and a rough outline of a woman as darkness envelopes her, bringing her down.

## Chapter Fourteen
# SYLVIE

Hours pass unnoticed as I lose myself in my art while music surrounds me. Slipknot, Five Finger Death Punch, and others set the mood while I paint.

The faint sound of a doorbell under the loud music catches my attention. I lay my brush and palette down before answering the front door. Two uniformed policemen stand before me. My skin chills, and the hairs on the back of my neck stand up. Bile climbs my throat as the memory of the night Omar died flashes to mind.

"Ma'am..." the older, slim, salt-and-pepper-haired officer greets.

"Come in," I rasp, trying to collect myself.

*Lidia? When did I last hear from Lidia? What were her plans for tonight?*

"I need to turn off the music." I excuse myself, scurrying back to my art room, silencing the playlist on my cell phone. Deafening silence fills the large, empty space. I look to the officers as they take in the empty interior. "Now, how can I help you?" my voice cracks.

The younger officer smirks. "We received a noise complaint from your neighbor."

*It's not Lidia. She's fine.*

Shock floods me then morphs to embarrassment, horror, and mortification.

"We could hear your music in the driveway," the young, hot cop with a badge reading "Kirshner" informs me.

"Crud!" I move to the new wall console control for the speakers. "I didn't know the pool speakers were on. I'm so sorry." My fingers point to each button on the system as I frantically search for the outdoor speakers. "The system was installed today, and it's my first time using it." I turn to face the men. "I promise it won't happen again."

Realizing Five Finger Death Punch's *Burn MF* played moments ago, my hand covers my mouth, and my eyes grow wide. The sound and lyrics are very inappropriate for non-metal fans to hear.

*What will my new neighbors think of me?*

"Ma'am are you the homeowner?" the older officer with a badge reading "Calderon" inquires.

"Yes. I have paperwork over here on the countertop." Sensing the empty home sends up red flags, I retrieve the documents as I continue, "My new furniture arrives in the morning."

The men look at one another then back to me. "Keep it down," Officer Calderon instructs.

"And apologize to your new neighbors," Officer Kirshner adds, with a wink and a sexy smirk.

I walk behind them to the door and let them out. I watch

as they pull from the curb at the end of my driveway, giving them a wave before I shut and lock the door.

*Way to go, Sylvie. Get it together. First day of your new life and you've already been approached by law enforcement.*

*Chapter Fifteen*
# STEPHEN

I recognize *Closer* by Nine Inch Nails playing loudly in the backyard as we approach the large ranch in an upper-middle class neighborhood.

We ring the bell twice and pound a fist upon the heavy wooden door. I'm sure we can't be heard over the music.

Eventually, the door swings open, and a stunning woman in denim overalls splattered with paint in every color of the rainbow stands before us, a gun-metal gray paint smudge upon her face where a finger must have touched her cheek. Scanning quickly, I notice paint on the bandana in her hair and speckles of paint splattered on her right shoulder. She strikes quite an image with her shiny, golden-sun-kissed skin, baggy overalls, and a tight white tank top beneath.

I thought I'd seen it all in my time on the force. She's a disheveled mess. A sexy, metal-loving, disheveled mess.

"Ma'am..." Fredrik greets.

"Come in," she rasps.

I scan the large open floorplan, finding her alone in an oddly empty space.

"I need to turn off the music," she excuses herself, scurrying back to the art easel, silencing the playlist on her cell phone. Silence fills the empty space. "Now, how can I help you?" her voice cracks.

I smirk. "We received a noise complaint from your neighbor."

Embarrassment evident on her face, her hand covers her mouth, and her eyes grow wide.

"We could hear your music in the driveway," I inform her.

"Crud!" She moves to the wall control for the speakers. "I didn't know the pool speakers were on. I'm so sorry." Her fingers point to each button on the system as she frantically searches for the outdoor speakers. "The system was installed today, and it's my first time using it." She turns to face us. "I promise it won't happen again."

"Ma'am are you the homeowner?" Fredrik inquires.

"Yes. I have paperwork over here on the countertop." She retrieves the documents. "My new furniture arrives in the morning."

I look at Fredrik then back to her. "Keep it down," I instruct. "And apologize to your new neighbors," I add with a wink.

She walks behind us to the door and lets us out. She watches as we pull from the curb at the end of the driveway, giving us a wave before she shuts the door.

---

## Later

. . .

"Fredrik, go home to your wife and kids," I call to my partner across our joined desks. "I'll write the report. Besides, it's the end of our shift. You should be there when your kids wake up." I'm already pulling up the driver's license of our last call, the noise complaint. He doesn't argue, quickly leaving before another call comes in.

While filling out the report, I see her birthday. Quickly, I do the math. *Wow. I would never have guessed it. Wait until I tell Fredrik.* I would have put her at 35, not a day over 38. *She looks fantastic for 42. Hmm. Intriguing. Good for her; she seems to enjoy life. This is why I should never judge a book by its cover.*

She's a little minx.

## Chapter Sixteen
# SYLVIE

The next morning, I happen to spot a cute little popcorn shop as I walk toward my car. *I love popcorn.* I step inside and buy a couple of bags of assorted flavors. I can't help myself; I purchase a large tin with three sections of different flavors. I smile, and my insides warm at my plans to drop it by the police station. *Come to think of it, I'd better get two tins, one for the day shift and one for the night shift.* I also grab a medium bag of the cheese and caramel mixture for the dispatchers. *Hopefully, in doing so, there will be some left for Officer Kirshner and Officer Calderon's shift.* It's a small I'm-sorry-for-being-a-nuisance and thank-you-for-keeping-our-community-safe token of my appreciation.

---

My stomach turns as I park my car. Suddenly, I feel like I might be sick. *Why am I acting this way? I'm simply treating the local station to popcorn, nothing more. No one needs to know that young hottie and the silver fox have been on my mind constantly since they left my place last night.*

I quell my nerves before I load the popcorn in both of my arms. I didn't think this through; it's too much to carry in one trip. Before I can return one of the large canisters to my trunk, a male voice offers to help me. I accept his assistance, explain why I'm here, and he escorts me into the station.

"Hi. I'm a local resident," I tell the women at the front desk. "I've brought popcorn for everyone."

At the mention of food, two nearby officers move closer. I fight the urge to chuckle and continue my explanation.

"I have a tub for the day shift and another for the night shift." I set the two canisters on the counter. "I even have two bags for the dispatchers."

"Oh, wow," the desk clerk smiles. "I'd better label these. In fact, I may need to hide the one for the night shift, or there will be nothing left for them."

I want to explain it's important that the night shift get popcorn since they are the reason, I wanted to get the gift in the first place.

"Who should I say these are from?" she asks, pen in hand.

"Sylvie Rice," I answer before I can think better of it. "Wait. No. Just say a local community member brought them in. They won't need to know my name."

"Gotcha," she winks. "Thanks for this."

## Chapter Seventeen
# SYLVIE

Today, I plan to add another toy to my garage. Excitement pumps through my veins as I pull into the dealership on Merle Hay Road. Unlike the two other times, today, I visit during business hours.

I slide my fingers along the trunk, the driver's door, and the hood. I pause in front to admire the sleek, little red sports car convertible.

"She's a beauty," a male voice calls, "isn't she?"

"Nope. *He's* an 18-year-old boy dressed in a tux on prom night. He's desperate to look the regal part but itching to go have some fun and take off his tux jacket and bowtie."

The salesman smirks, believing he's got me on the hook for an easy sale. "It's ready to drive home today."

"No, but it will be," I counter.

He tilts his head, amused a woman believes she knows more about cars then men, and places his hand on my back.

"Honey, I promise it's ready. I'll even throw in two years of oil changes and tire rotations."

*Honey? Honey! Did this man just call me honey?*

I stride towards the showroom, my thoughts stormy as I rage over his demeaning words and his hand upon my back like he knows me. It's one thing to insinuate I need a spouse for such a big purchase; it's another to use that language with me.

At the reception area, I ask, "May I speak to a manager?" When I'm directed to the salesman approaching the door that I already spoke to, I shake my head. "I need his supervisor."

Judging by the receptionist's reaction, she knows what I'm upset about. "Follow me."

"How may I help you?" the supervisor greets, extending his hand across the desk.

"I'm here to buy a car," I begin, causing his smile to widen. "And a salesman of yours called me 'honey.' He doesn't know me, and I'm offended he spoke to me in that manner and placed his hands on me."

"I'm sorry that happened..."

I interrupt. "Sorry doesn't work for me. I'm here to purchase a car with cash today, and your skeevy employee gives me the creeps."

"This is not his first complaint, but it will be the last. You have my word on that," he states, his phone in his hand to text.

I furrow my brow as I assess his sincerity. My gut tells me he'll be true to his word. I nod my head, ready to move on.

"I'm interested in the little red Miata on the lot," I

inform him. "One tire doesn't match. If you throw in four new tires, I will pay full asking price in cash today."

I leave the lot; my new toy being delivered to my home later today with a full tank of gas and four new tires. I'm giddy with pride. I'm proving to be the strong, assertive woman that I once was and am striving, again, to be.

## Chapter Eighteen
# SYLVIE

"How much has your new guitar hobby cost?" Lidia asks on her next weekend visit home.

It's really none of her business. It's something I enjoy, and I have the money to buy myself nice things. There is a difference in instruments, and I didn't buy from the cheaper end of the spectrum.

"I know it's not my business," Lidia states. "I see you now have a Fender next to the Les Paul."

"I'll just say there are many more expensive guitars than my Fender Telecaster," I share. "I can always sell it for good money if I ever stop playing."

"I don't want you to stop playing," she quickly shares. "It only made me think of your future new hobbies and how much they might cost; you may not stick with them."

"Honey, I told you. Your father had both of us taken care of," I remind her. "Come with me."

"Where are we going?" she asks before she stands to follow me.

"I want to show you the financials..."

"Nope." She quickly and boldly says, "I don't want to know."

"Yet you are worried about me spending $1,500 on a new guitar." I raise an eyebrow at her.

"I know you said it's more than I have in my trust fund. I just can't help but worry. You've purchased new cars, a new house, new furniture, and all the decorations," she explains.

"If I told you it's more than four times your trust fund, would you stop worrying?" I offer.

Lidia coughs caught off guard. I've tried to share the financials with her many times; she is adamant she doesn't want to know. A part of her is worried, and I need to calm those nerves once and for all.

She clears her throat. "That much?"

I nod.

"Wow!" She stands, taking my hand in hers. "I guess I shouldn't worry about you spending $2,000 on your new hobby then."

We chuckle.

"I don't plan on spending it all," I promise.

"It's your money to spend any way you want. I just wanted to make sure there was enough as I plan on you living for many decades." She tilts her head to the side.

"I'm living off of the interest," I share. "You'll inherit..."

"No... Nope..." she shouts, her hands flying to cover her ears. "Do. Not. Finish. That. Statement."

I nod. She's right. It's only been a year since she lost her father. She shouldn't think about losing me, too.

*Chapter Nineteen*

# STEPHEN

"Oh my!" A loud female voice catches my attention to my left. "You're certainly proud of your member, aren't you?" Her laughter tickles the air.

I blink, not believing my eyes. The woman we made a noise complaint on last week, emerges from the big cat building. Her cheeks are bright pink, and she covers her mouth as she laughs. She pauses mere feet away, quickly typing on her cell phone before tucking it into her denim cutoffs. When she looks up, she immediately notices us.

She lifts her chin in our direction. "Officers."

"Hello, ma'am," Fredrik greets.

"I have to know. What was the conversation you were having?" I motion to the big cat paddock she just exited.

She rubs her forehead, wiping sweat from her brow on this warm June night.

"I tried to get a photo of me with the lion," she confesses. "He was only interested in cleaning his privates right by the glass." She chuckles. "Well, I guess I'm assuming he was cleaning and not..." She clears her throat. "Certainly not a PG-13 exhibit at the moment," she laughs.

"What a hoot," Fredrik chuckles when she walks away. "And don't think I haven't seen you light up at the sight of her twice now."

"Fuck." I know I'll be the butt of his jokes now. He won't move on; he'll pester me about her every chance he gets.

---

## Sylvie

*What have I done?*

I stand in the kitchen of my new house, observing two dogs scurrying about, sniffing every corner as they explore their new home.

My plan for the day was to pick up my new Basset Hound puppy from the breeder. Bocephus, Bo for short, is 8 pounds of the most adorable puppy I've ever seen. His large paws pad along as his long, droopy ears drag to the floor.

On my way home, with Bo in his carrier, I felt guilty for purchasing a puppy when so many dogs wait in pounds for new homes. With each passing mile, my guilt grew.

Hagrid, the name given to him by his former family, is a mixed breed. The employees at the Animal Rescue League guessed he's part Rottweiler. He's 5 years old, and his family moved into a new rental with a strict "no pets" policy.

As Hagrid sniffs high and low, Bo trots behind him, sniffing the floor. When Hagrid laps water from the small dish I purchased for my new puppy, I realize I need to make another trip to the pet store. The tiny food and water dishes will not work for both dogs. Hagrid will need his own set, bigger kennel, and larger, soft bed.

I only have one leash, so I can't take both with me to shop at PetSmart. There's no way I can leave a new puppy alone in my absence. I'll need Bo in his kennel then have to trust that Hagrid is house trained. Clearly, I didn't think all of this through.

Deciding to postpone my trip to the pet store for an hour or two, I pull out my phone and send a Snap of my new fur babies to Lidia. She often asked for a dog growing up, but Omar strongly opposed it.

Immediately, I laugh as I answer her incoming video call.

## Chapter Twenty
# SYLVIE

Slowly, I'm decorating my new home, making it my own. All my new furniture graces the place. Now, I'm purchasing decorative pillows and items for the shelves and walls.

I've purchased many things in the past two weeks from Amazon and other online retailers. I know the UPS guy by name. It's not uncommon for me to receive at least three deliveries in a week. He teases me about having a shopping addiction and promises to report me before I'm too far gone.

I move my box cutter along the seam of the third box to arrive today. With each box, I feel the excitement of Christmas morning in my youth. Although I purchase the items online, by the time they arrive, I forget what should be inside. This box contains a chenille blanket for the back of my sofa. I imagine I'll use it when winter arrives.

My stomach growls, reminding me it's lunch time. I groan; meals for one are a challenge. When I cook, I have leftovers for another meal or two, and most of the leftovers lose their taste the next day.

Recently, I decided to try new restaurants for lunch. It reminds me of the mother-daughter lunches Lidia and I had one Saturday a month before she entered high school and got too busy. Now in college, we enjoy meals out when I visit her in Iowa City.

Eating alone bothered me the first time, but now, I figure I'm rewarding myself with takeout or delivery. I've become a foodie of sorts, trying new places and new menu items. I share each of my lunch endeavors via Snapchat with Lidia.

---

It's a perfect day. The sun is out, and it's not too windy for a top-down ride in my Miata to pick up take-out. I plan to dine on a park bench since I can't fit a lawn chair into the tiny trunk of this car.

I choose a tiny tenderloin restaurant on the south side. It's been featured as a stop of Presidential candidates before the caucuses, so I'm excited to check it out.

I let the sounds and smells of the restaurant stimulate visions in my mind to later paint on my canvas. If that doesn't inspire me, eating at the park allows nature to spark my creative juices.

I lean on the edge of my car, watching runners, walkers, and bikers on the trail around Grey's Lake as I slowly enjoy my meal. With each bite, I grow more anxious to return home to my studio and record the senses of today's culinary adventure.

The greasy smell of the restaurant evokes the image of

sharp points, maybe geometric shapes on my canvas. The sandwich reminds me of a small farm town. It's simple; a pork tenderloin and bun, yet it doesn't lack taste or charm. I think I'll paint a rural community this afternoon.

At home, I quickly grab a water before I address my blank canvas with my paintbrush in hand. As is always the case, butterflies flutter in my belly before I make the first brushstroke. I take a deep breath and begin.

When I yawn for the second time, I take a step back to admire my progress then glance at my phone screen. *It's 10.* I've painted for nine hours. At this knowledge, my stomach growls, and my bladder signals it's well past a bathroom break.

As I clean my brushes, I decide I need to set another alarm on my phone like I do for lunch. It will signal, "Time for a dinner break!" each day. I often lose all track of time in my studio; I'm blessed that way.

## Chapter Twenty-One
# SYLVIE

My air-conditioned house or even the swimming pool would feel good about now. It's 86 degrees, and I'm walking on hot pavement in downtown Des Moines. I offered to meet Lidia and a couple of her friends to browse the art at this year's Art Festival. I must admit, I had no idea how hot it would be at this time of the evening; I might not have agreed to go if I did.

At our meeting spot, I wipe my brow as I scan the crowd for any sign of my daughter. There's a huge gathering. This annual event makes the news every year; it wasn't until Lidia suggested it that I chose to come down and check it out for myself. Maybe I'll find some things for the new house.

Lidia and her friend's approach with wide smiles, giggling and whispering. Though I strain, I cannot hear what they are going on about. I do hear all of them *shhh* each other as they wave in my direction.

"Mrs. Rice, you look amazing!" Lidia's best friend announces.

"I'm so glad you joined us," one of her friends greets.

"I don't want to ruin your time together," I state.

"Nonsense! We'll look around, try some food, and have a great time," another friend assures me.

We make our way down one side of the street, moving from vendor to vendor. I find so many interesting pieces and mediums.

"Mom, you should set up a space here next year," Lidia encourages, nudging me with her elbow.

"I bet the booth space is expensive, and the event is popular enough they're sure to have a wait list." I fiddle with copper bracelets on display.

"I'm sure it's cheaper than the new Fender guitar you bought last month," Lidia chides. "Anyway, your art is worth as much as your new hobby, isn't it?"

"We'll see," I placate her, walking to the next booth, wanting the topic to change.

"Hey!" one of the girls whisper-yells at the group. "There he is again."

I attempt to follow her pointing, but I can't see through the crowd from where I stand.

"Stop!" Lidia reprimands.

"He can see you pointing," another hisses.

I crane my neck, but the crowd is too large for me to know which guy they are infatuated with. I love it. They're young, dynamic, single ladies. Surely any guy attending the art festival would be worthy of them.

"Duck!" Lidia yells.

The four girls bend their knees to fade into the crowd.

"Who are we hiding from?" I ask, standing above them once again, craning my neck for a better view.

"Shh!" the girls demand in unison.

"The cop," one whispers, causing me to believe he's close by.

I shake my head, not seeing any police officers. I wonder... No, it couldn't be the cop that called on my house. I smile at my silly thought.

"What?" Lidia asks, slowly standing up beside me.

"I find it funny that you're acting this way about a policeman after I told you about my interaction with hot cops at my house," I murmur, not wanting all the girls to hear me.

"What did your hot cops look like?" one of my daughter's friends asks.

I bite my lip to hide my grin.

"What were their names? You saw their badges, right?" Lidia asks, drawing all the girls' attention.

"Officer Kirshner was the young hottie," I share. "And Officer Calderon was the silver fox."

"OMG! Mrs. Rice..." one of the girls giggles.

Lidia's fingers fly on her phone screen. "Is this him?" She shoves her phone much too close to my face.

I place my hand on hers, lowering her phone to the proper viewing distance, then freeze. With wide eyes, I nod.

"That's young hottie," I state.

"That's the cop. He's right over there," Lidia points.

I look but can't find any cops in that direction. I continue to look to the left and right, finding nothing.

"I'd say he's a silver fox," Lidia chuckles.

I turn to find the gang admiring Officer Calderon's photo on a Des Moines Police Department press release.

"They both were at your house?" Lidia asks, disbelieving.

I nod. "I told you, I should have gotten his number for you," I remind her. "Capital H-O-T, right?"

All the girls nod.

"And I bumped into the two of them at Zoo Brew, too." I smirk as the girls stare at me in awe.

While I continue to look at art, it's clear the girls make finding the cop priority number one with art now second place.

## Chapter Twenty-Two
# SYLVIE

I love my life, I feel guilty for saying it with the loss of Omar, but I really love my life. I'm still adjusting to my time alone each night, slowly I'm getting the hang of it. I make the most of it by playing my guitars or painting.

I remind myself with Lidia at college and Omar working late, I spent most evenings alone. Of course, my mind wanders during these times to Omar during trials "sleeping at the office". It's in the silence and darkness at night that my former life and relationship with Omar haunt me. I was so naïve and blind. Perhaps I longed for ignorance. I didn't look, I didn't ask, and I didn't care.

*Wait. What? I cared. I fucking cared. Didn't I? I mean, I loved Omar, I kept the house for him, and I raised our daughter. Maybe I didn't ask some questions I should have. Maybe I looked the other way. Maybe I allowed our marriage to become friendship. A don't ask, don't tell, sexless friendship. Man, I was such an idiot.*

*Not again. Never again. I plan to live, to engage, to experience everything for the rest of my life.*

---

Sitting on the floor, I prop myself against the sofa, my iPad in hand. I open the browser to begin my search. One dog on the sofa and the other beside me, I type "current trends in dating." It's been decades since I dated; I'm not ready yet, but I need to brush up. What seems like millions of sites appear before me. I scroll past the top five which are ads and click on "dating apps."

The first one is Bumble. *It sounds like a bee.* Next. Faith-based. Next. Tinder. *Hmm, don't you start a fire with that?* Next. Silver— *Uh-huh, I'm not that old. Do people really use these apps to date? This is not for me.*

Next, I type in "modern dating terms." Hook up. *Do I want to hookup?* Jekylling, Elsa'd, Rossing, Keanu-ing, whelming, dog fishing, dial toning, flat lining, and stashing. *I will need a handheld dictionary with me on dates. When did dating become so difficult? When I'm ready, I just want to meet, talk, and if we like each other, to go on a date.*

Continuing my research, I read extensively about waxing and manscaping. Next, I learn about piercings. When the first sketch pops up, I decide I'm not ready to learn about dating. I shut the browser and turn off my tablet. Now, I'm scared to death at the thought of dating. Perhaps I'll wait a couple months before I research more.

## Chapter Twenty-Three
# SYLVIE

The next weekend, sitting across from Lidia at a favorite restaurant, the waiter delivers our fried pickle spears appetizer and offers to bring us two more drinks. We've covered the usual: her classes, my art, her activities, the weather, and plans for the rest of the week.

Now's my chance to ask for advice. "I've been researching dating," I blurt.

"Why?" she asks between bites.

"Don't you think it's time I consider it?" I defend.

"No. I'm not asking why you're dating," Lidia explains. "Why are you researching?"

"A lot has changed in the over 20 years since I last dated." While waiting for her comments, I enjoy another bite of fried pickle.

"Yes, it has, but the internet's not where you should research. Did porn pop up?" Her smile is wide as if she knows all about my little research fiasco.

"Yes. It was just a sketch, but I immediately knew I was in over my head." *I scheduled this luncheon in order to ask for dating advice, so here it goes.* "Have you ever seen a pierced penis?"

Lidia coughs, having swallowed wrong.

I push her tea glass towards her. "Well, have you?"

"No," she scoffs. "Have you?"

I shake my head. "I glanced at the sketch before I freaked and closed the browser."

Lidia fans her red face, eyes wide, worried about this topic, apparently.

"What do you know about manscaping?" I blurt.

"Mom!" Lidia scans nearby tables to see if anyone overheard me. "Stop doing research."

"If I date, it's important I know what I'm in for," I tell her.

"You won't encounter a pierced cock or manscaping on your first date," she whispers.

I raise an eyebrow at her.

"I mean," she clarifies, "that I hope you won't on your first date. Or fifth date for that matter." She scans the restaurant again. "What brought this on?"

"I've read about them in romance books," I confess. "I looked them up, so I'd understand what I was reading."

Lidia shakes her head at me.

After chewing another bite, I move on to my next question. "Where do you propose I meet potential dates?"

"Church, the grocery store, the YMCA before or after your yoga class, or while walking in your neighborhood," Lidia suggests. "It's a long process, and you don't want to use dating apps." She sips from her iced tea glass before continuing. "Have I used one? Yes, but most of the time, I don't. I meet guys at parties or at bars."

"I met your father at a college homecoming bonfire."

She nods. "I know. You've both told me the story. My advice? Go to events in the community."

"Just so you know, I'm not in any hurry," I clarify.

"Okay, but you deserve to meet others and create new relationships," she states. "Put yourself out there. Go to events, meet people, and have fun. That's when potential dates will pop up."

I smile, proud of my daughter. Her advice is solid. I purse my lips, realizing both Edith and Lidia believe I should to prioritize my need to meet more people by attending events.

## Chapter Twenty-Four
# STEPHEN

It's times like this that make me wonder if the overtime is worth it. Fredrik really needs the extra money, so I do it to keep him company. The heat from the pavement penetrates the soles of my black work boots. We need to find a piece of cardboard to stand on like we do in the winter.

It's six, and the sun is slowly sliding from the sky. A high of 100 degrees today means we're still in the upper 90s this late in the afternoon. For the hundredth time, I wipe the sweat from my brow, my nose, and cheeks. I berate myself for not drinking more water today.

It feels like the Kevlar is fusing with my chest; no amount of shade helps tonight without a breeze. I return my thoughts to my task for the evening. I scan the mall parking lot, making sure this bike night runs smoothly.

The lot is finally full; the crowd doubled in the last hour. I remind myself I'm here to watch the people, not admire the bikes. My scan of the event stops on a cluster gathered around bikes near the stage, where a local cover band sets up.

My eyes look for any sign of conflict. I crane my neck, looking to the center of the group.

"I'm gonna check this out," I tell my partner, my chin motioning towards the growing crowd.

I make my way toward the stage and walk up from the opposite side of the group. It seems they're admiring a bike. A tall, slender woman stands at the handlebars, her back toward me. She wears skin-tight jeans and a tight, black tank top. I don't approach. Keeping my distance, I monitor the situation.

"You're staring at the bike, right?" Fredrik teases beside me. I didn't even hear him approach.

It's at that moment that the crowd steps back, and the woman turns.

*What the fuck? It's her. I don't believe it.*

"Now I know why you're staring," Fredrik teases. "Damn man..."

"Right?" I groan.

It's Sylvie Rice. Again. I'd never seen the woman before her noise complaint. Now, she's popping up everywhere. The orange Harley Davidson logo on her tank top draws my eye to her breasts. The tight jeans and black biker boots only add to her allure.

"You're drooling." Fredrik nudges my shoulder with his.

"I'm looking at the bike," I lie then move my eyes in its direction.

She stands beside a charcoal bike with the metal logo on the tank. Below it, a moth or butterfly spreads its wings while sitting on a cocoon. I find myself wondering if she painted it herself as I know she's an artist.

A guy points to the art then the area above his old lady's heart. They must be contemplating a tattoo. Ms. Rice nods and pulls out her phone, and they exchange information. The local cover band now plays 70s and 80s rock on the nearby stage.

Amidst the public here that doesn't ride, the weekend riders, and the hardcore bikers, she seems to fit right in. That night at her new house, I thought she was a sexy loon. While typing the report, I decided she was the typical housewife. Now, I'm not sure how to label her. *She's an enigma.*

"Yeah," Fredrik agrees.

*Did I say that out loud?*

"Come on, lover boy." Again, he nudges my shoulder; this time, I follow him.

Back at our central location, I try my best to spread my attention over the entire crowd. *She rides a bike.* I shake away the thought. *Work. I need to work.* I scan the crowd, not allowing myself to look in her direction. It's difficult, there's something about her that calls to me.

I slowly, intentionally, slide my eyes from one bike to the next, counting to three in my head before moving on. With every breath, I will myself not to look back in her direction. I move my eyes like a typewriter from right to left, only halfway, then left to right.

## Chapter Twenty-Five
# SYLVIE

*Damn, it's hot.* I should have worn shorts, but I wanted to fit in at my first bike event. I worried I wouldn't be taken seriously in my denim shorts and biker boots.

My research on bike events online did not prepare me for the crowd that flocks to my bike before I get my helmet off. I fight the urge to tell them to keep their hands off my bike. I answer many questions about my ride, where I found it, and where I live. It seems for every person that walks away, two more approach. Eventually, I excuse myself to walk around, leaving the group with my bike.

*Holy hotness!* My eyes land on two officers leaning on a barricade. To my surprise, it's the silver fox and the young hottie.

Officer Kirshner strikes a commanding presence, his skin glistening in the heat. His bulky muscles spill out of his uniform shirt, his hands grasping his bullet-proof vest at his collarbone. It's easy to see his upper arms and thighs match his visible muscles.

He's like a red popsicle. I long to lick, suck, and bite into him. *Stop that! Get a hold of yourself, woman.* He's much too young. His partner is my age, and the silver fox is *fine*. He could pass for that actor Harrington on the TV show S.W.A.T. As handsome as he is, my eyes keep migrating back to Officer Kirshner.

I hide my smile when, at my approach, Officer Calderon nudges Officer Kirshner, motioning toward me.

"Are you two stalking me?" I ask, hands on my hips. "First, you take the disturbance call to my house. Then, it was maybe a coincidence to see you at Zoo Brew. But here, tonight? This crosses the line."

"We're just doing our job," the silver fox states.

"Uh-huh." I shake my head.

"Thanks for the popcorn," the young hottie smirks. "Some might think you coming to our place of work was stalking." His smile widens as he taunts.

"Just a citizen thanking her local law enforcement. I bought enough for everyone. And they weren't supposed to put my name as the donor." I move my fists from my hips, crossing my arms across my chest.

I notice Officer Kirshner's eyes hone in on my chest with my movements. My skin prickles under his gaze.

"No. Really," Officer Kirshner adds. "Thank you for the popcorn. It's rare that we get a treat like that."

"You are welcome." I smile. "I best get back to my bike." I glance over my shoulder at the crowd behind me. "This is probably not the place to let them think I'm friendly with the po-po."

As I walk back to view other bikes, I chide myself. *Way to play it cool, dummy. Do they still refer to police as po-po?* I never thought in a million years that I'd run into those two again.

As I try to play it cool, viewing other motorcycles, I send a Snapchat to Lidia with the words, "Guess who I bumped into at bike night."

Walking from bike to bike, I occasionally glance in the direction of the officers. I find Officer Kirshner's often looking at me. I'm not sure what I should make of his attention. It's foreign, and I like it.

## Chapter Twenty-Six
## SYLVIE

While a late-July thunderstorm brews outside in the night, I sit in front of my laptop, hands in my hair. I opened YouTube on the browser minutes ago. I want to follow through on the challenge Edith put out for me this month. I want to share my music but am afraid of live audiences. By posting a video of my music online, I can share while avoiding the crowd for now.

Slowly, I will my fingers to create an account. It's not the YouTube channel that I'm anxious about; it's putting myself out there for comments. I'm not delusional. I know there will be both good and bad comments, and I'm not sure I want to hear the public's feedback. I enjoy playing; it's something I do for myself. By uploading a video, I'll open myself to others, and that's scary and exciting at the same time.

I strum my fingers on the table as I wait for my video to upload and process. *I'm really doing this.*

I begin to contemplate the number of views I might get.

Lidia will watch it, perhaps even a few of her friends. *Ten. I bet I get a total of 10 views.* I remind myself that I'm not doing this for the views, likes, or shares. *I'm challenging myself to try something new; and that is reward enough.*

After the video processes, I watch it from start to finish two times. One of the many things I learned at my Apple Store class was to send and receive texts on all three of my devices. I copy the direct link and text it to Lidia. Not bad for my first video upload. I'll need to position my camera a little tighter on my upper body and guitar next time.

*Next time.* I giggle, proud I'm considering there will be a next time.

---

I'm in the backyard playing fetch with the dogs the next morning when Lidia calls.

"Mom!" she squeals and continues to speak unintelligibly.

"Calm down," I instruct. "What's wrong?"

Still squealing, she repeats, "Look at your video views!"

"Why?" I stupidly ask, moving inside towards my laptop.

I hear her talking to people on her end of the phone call. Before she answers, my browser refreshes, and I have 5.7 thousand views and over 200 subscribers.

"That's way more than 10," I murmur.

"What?" Lidia asks.

I forgot she was on the phone. "Wow! Lidia, I expected like 10 views. I mean 10 total views." I place my free hand on my chest. "What happened?"

"You're a hit! That's what happened," she congratulates. "I viewed it, showed it to my roommate, and shared it with the girls. From there, it snowballed. I told you how good you are. Now the world can see it, too."

"I don't know about the world…"

"Mom, you're talented. I bet you have twice as many views by tomorrow." She pauses to speak to someone in the background. "I mean, it hasn't even been 24 hours yet."

Her excitement, even over the phone, is contagious. Others like my guitar playing. My heart races as I plot to record my next song to post.

## Chapter Twenty-Seven
# SYLVIE

Days later, I pick up my ringing cell phone with "unknown caller" across the screen. "Hello?" I greet.

"Hi. Is this Sylvia Rice?" the female voice asks.

"Sylvie," I correct. "Yes."

"My name is Dawn," she starts. "I fell in love with one of your paintings while visiting a church member in the nursing home today." She pauses for a moment as I wonder where this is going. "I asked the staff, and they gave me your name."

"Okay..." I draw out.

"Well, I'd love to schedule a meeting, maybe for lunch or drinks."

"Okay..." I repeat.

"Are you available tomorrow?" she excitedly asks.

"I guess," I hedge.

"Let's say 11 at the Hy-Vee grocery store on Fleur," she suggests. "They have a full-service restaurant and bar inside."

"Okay," I mutter.

"Good. Then, I will see you tomorrow at 11," Dawn states then ends the call.

I stand, phone in hand, disbelieving. I can't wrap my mind around it; I replay the conversation in my mind. I guess I'm meeting a woman named Dawn at 11 tomorrow at the grocery store to discuss the paintings I purged and donated to a nearby nursing home.

---

"Do you belong to any clubs or charities?" Dawn, sitting across from me, begins, excitement bubbling in her every word.

"No," I confess.

"I'm on the Juvenile Diabetes Research Foundation board and am involved with the Variety Club," she shares, eyes bright, smiling wide. "I wondered if you might donate a painting for the upcoming JDRF and Variety Club auctions?"

Her smile… This woman's smile should be bottled up and sold. It, matched with her personality, draws me to the vivacious lady.

"Of course, if you think someone would bid on it. I doubt it would bring much money," I admit.

"We set the minimum bid, and the community often pays two to three times what the item's worth," Dawn boasts. Her contagious, megawatt excitement begins to light a flame within me.

"Would you like to join me for the next planning meeting? We can use all the help we can get," she asks hopefully.

Edith and Lidia's constant prompting to make friends and get involved in the community comes to mind. "I'll give it a try." I nod, a wide smile on my face. "Honestly, the works I donated to the senior center are not..." I search for the words, attempting not to belittle my donation. "My better works, I kept."

"Might I see them?" my new acquaintance, Dawn, asks eagerly.

*Who could refuse her?* "My studio is in my home," I explain.

"Could I follow you home and take a peek?" Her eyes brighten at the thought of seeing more.

## Chapter Twenty-Eight
# SYLVIE

I'm not sure why I didn't object. I stand in my driveway as Dawn pulls into my neighbor's driveway to park. *Why is she parking there? My neighbor will not like it if my guests park there.* I open my mouth to protest.

"Hello, neighbor," she beams, both arms waving at me.

My brow crinkles. *Is she crazy? I must be crazy, allowing this loon to follow me home.*

"That's my house." She points to the house next to mine.

I look from her to the house and back.

"It's kismet," she cheers, clapping, smiling widely.

"You live in that house?" I seek to understand.

"Yes," she reiterates, her head bobbing. "We're neighbors."

As we step into my house, she confesses, "I'm the one that called the police about the noise."

She doesn't apologize to me as I stand dumbfounded in

my kitchen. I don't blame her. I was playing my music too loud that night.

"Sylvie?" Dawn prompts, pulling me from my stupor.

"My studio is in here." I swing my arm to the four-season room.

"I knew it!" Dawn claps her hands in front of her face. "I had a feeling it'd be this good." She stands, head tilted in front of my easel.

"That's not finished," I inform as I pull a cloth sheet off my paintings leaning in the corner.

"Oh, my," she gasps.

"These are my most recent," I boast.

"And you'd donate two of these?" She asks again the question she brought up over lunch.

I nod. "Any of these," I vow. I don't share that my most prized paintings are down on shelves in the storage room. "Do you think they'd help you raise money?"

"Of course, they'll be great silent auction items," Dawn promises. "I can't believe you aren't attending art fairs or selling them in area stores."

I'm not used to sharing my artwork with anyone. In fact, it's only recently that I've begun to share it with Lidia. I'm as excited as I am scared. I'm not sure I'm ready for public input—good or bad.

"Which two are you willing to donate?" she asks.

"You'll know what your guests might be interested in," I state, wanting her to make the decision.

Dawn's excitement bounces like a red rubber ball off of the walls as she inspects each canvas before leaning it against an open space along the wall.

"I think this one for the JDRF auction and this one for the Variety Club."

I nod.

"Our guests will love these," Dawn promises. "You should approach stores at Valley Junction about carrying your art."

I'm silent; I'm not sure what to say. I'm scared. Sharing music is one thing. Sharing my painting is another. I'm not used to sharing my art; as of today, it's public.

"I can't wait for my friend, Theo, to see these," Dawn continues. "We are on both boards together. She'll love these. Thank you."

## Chapter Twenty-Nine
# SYLVIE

I'm five minutes early as I exit my Miata at the meeting location in the Valley West Mall parking lot. I investigated the Miata club online, and now that I am here, I'm rethinking this event. I hoped I'd meet some new friends; I had no idea exactly how big this club was.

I walk past several cars toward the large group gathered nearby.

"Welcome," a female voice greets. "You must be Sylvie."

I nod, shaking her hand. I'm introduced to several couples, waving at many more, then it's time to hit the road. I climb back into the driver's seat, falling in line behind a black convertible.

I notice, of the cars in front of me and behind, that I'm the only single driver. I guess I'll meet twice as many people when we reach our destination.

I give myself permission to sing along with the radio as the warm summer air whips by.

Arriving in Clear Lake, we visit a tiny ice cream shop before parking in another area and walking several blocks to the lake's edge. In the July heat, the ice cream quickly melts. I use my napkins to wipe my brow several times and do my best to remain in the shade of nearby houses and trees.

I stand with a group of three couples, listening in on their conversation for a bit before they state it's time to return to our cars and hit the road.

"So, we just drive for two hours, visit, then drive two hours again?" I ask the couple I recently met.

"Sometimes, we stay overnight and have more time to visit," the woman states.

*These are NOT my people, and this is not my scene. What a waste of a Saturday.* I tried it but won't be returning. Instead of following in the long line of convertibles, I opt to take a different route through town. I'm on the interstate before the club arrives, and that allows me to drive the faster speeds I enjoy on my way home.

## Chapter Thirty
# SYLVIE

The next day, while I'm shopping at Scheel's, making my way around another circular clothing rack, I nearly bump into a young girl holding two t-shirts in front of her. I watch for a moment as she appraises both.

"Having trouble deciding?" I offer, and she turns to face me.

"Dad says," she begins, "that I can buy Mom one Chiefs shirt for her birthday."

"I see. I had trouble deciding, too." I motion to my armload of Chiefs attire. I place them on the shelf in the center of the rack. My cell phone buzzes with an incoming Snap from Lidia.

"Do you know how to use Snapchat?" I ask the little girl.

She smiles wide while nodding her head, her dark curls bouncing, so I extend my cell phone to her.

"My daughter downloaded the app and showed me how

to use it," I explain. "But I don't remember how to change the camera for a selfie."

"It's the rectangle here, with the arrows," she says as she taps it.

"Well, that was easy." I smile, taking my phone in hand. "Would you mind posing in a selfie to send to my daughter to prove I went shopping today?"

"Okay," she quickly agrees.

I snap our selfie and type a quick note on it. "Made a friend while shopping today."

"You should add some stickers," she suggests, so I squat beside her.

She deftly swipes through, finding a filter that adds "West Des Moines" and the date.

"Cool! Thank you."

She immediately returns to her impending decision.

"Here." I extend my hand with a 20-dollar bill I pulled from my purse.

"What's this?" she asks, staring at my extended hand.

"You helped me with Snapchat, and computer techs make good money. Now, you can buy your mom both of the Chiefs shirts." I wave the money in my hand towards her.

"Thanks." She grins, snags the bill, then proceeds to run to join her father who is standing nearby.

*This. Can. Not. Be. Happening.* I'm dumbfounded.

Leaning against a railing at the edge of the center aisle stands the two police officers. They're in street clothes, but I can easily tell it's them. *Is this more than a coincidence?*

As I load my selections back across my left arm, I frequently glance in their direction. The young girl hands her money to the silver fox then holds up both shirts for his approval. Both men then stare at me. While I can't read the silver fox's expression, the young hottie tries to hide his smile while shaking his head. When the silver fox beckons me with the raise of his chin, I slowly approach.

"You really didn't need to..." her father starts.

"She helped me with my phone," I explain. "IT people make good money." I smile, hoping I didn't overstep my bounds.

"I see," he mumbles.

"I'll pay for one shirt," the little girl pleads with her father. "And you'll pay for one shirt." Smiling, she anxiously awaits her father's approval.

"Let's put the $20 in your savings account, and I'll buy both shirts for your mom."

At his words, his daughter hops up and down, clapping before the two approach the cash registers nearby.

"Are you stalking me?" the young hottie teases.

"As you can see," I extend my armful, "I've been shopping longer than you've been here. Thus, you must be stalking me."

We stand quietly for a moment.

"So, the two of you are together even on your days off?" I inquire.

"No, we're not always together," he explains with a chuckle. "About once a month, I offer to watch his kids so he and his wife can spend some adult time together." His inquisitive eyes pierce mine.

*No way. Not only is the young hottie keeping the city safe, but he's also a caring family man. He's too perfect; he's too good to be true.*

He clears his throat, drawing my attention back. I find

myself staring at his extended hand with a white business card in it.

"What's this?" I ask.

"Well, if you take it," he pushes his hand and card closer to me, "it's my cell number. I thought maybe it'd be fun to get lunch or a coffee together."

"I see." I take the proffered card.

---

Sitting in the mall parking lot, I don't start my car. Instead, I text my daughter.

**Me: Need to meet ASAP; need advice**

At home, putting away my new clothes, she replies that she'll be here for dinner.

## Chapter Thirty-One
# SYLVIE

"What's with all the Amazon boxes?" Lidia asks, scanning the brown stacks along the wall by the front door.

I flip my wrist, signaling it's nothing. "I found a few items for the kitchen and some picture frames."

"Well, there are three new ones out on the front porch," Lidia informs, peering through the front window. Turning to me, she raises an eyebrow. "Is all this stuff making you happy? Or are you bored?" she asks, concern upon her face.

"I'm updating," I defend. "See for yourself; open them for me." I pass her the box cutter. "I'll fix iced tea."

Lidia opens each box, placing the items on the dining table. I return, handing her a tea glass garnished with a slice of lemon.

"I love these frames," Lidia says, running her fingers over the deep design in the wood. "And these new serving bowls will look great with your new dishes."

"I sent several photos to be printed," I inform. "I plan to display them throughout the house."

"These aren't for the house," Lidia teases, lifting one red Converse shoe from its package.

"It's part of my new wardrobe," I defend.

"Since we wear the same size, I might need to borrow these sometime." She smiles hopefully.

"A year ago, you wouldn't even consider borrowing from me," I remind her.

"So, that's a yes, I can borrow them?" she asks.

I nod, loving that my daughter approves of my new style.

"It's really starting to come together," Lidia agrees, looking around the space.

I need to start my planned conversation, but I chicken out. *Later. I will do it later.*

---

"Let's head out by the pool," I suggest. "Choose one of your playlists. I've turned on the outdoor speakers."

Bocephus floats on a foam mat as I sit near the edge of the pool, my feet beside him.

"Will Hagrid get in?" Lidia inquires.

"Sometimes he does. He usually gets wet then lays in the shade," I explain, my feet slowly moving the mat in the water. When I guide the mat close to us, she rubs his forehead between his long ears.

"You are the cutest, most spoiled puppy I've ever seen."

*Here's the moment. I can do this.*

"So, you know how I shared that I've run into that cop a

few times?" I pause, still not sure how to broach the subject of age.

"Yeah. Did you bump into him again?" she asks.

I can't fight the silly smile of a teenage girl that slips upon my face.

"Details," she orders.

I excuse myself to grab his business card.

## Chapter Thirty-Two
# SYLVIE

"Hmm..." Lidia twists her lips, staring at the business card Stephen handed me.

"Well?" I prompt.

"Well, I like it." She smiles, crossing her arms over her chest.

"Huh?"

"I'm just going by all you've told me. I've never met him, but he's smooth. He's put the ball in your court," she explains.

"What do you mean?"

"He's allowing you to contact him. He doesn't have your number. So, you have all the power." Lidia takes my hand in hers. "Do you like him?"

I shrug. She releases my hand, grabbing her cell phone.

"What are you doing? Don't text him!" I panic.

"Easy," she chides. "I wouldn't text him from my phone.

I'm looking him up; I need to see a picture of your young hottie again."

I lean into her side, looking over her shoulder.

"He's not on Facebook or Instagram," she tells me, her fingers flying over her screen. "We'll have to look to the internet."

"Holy shit!" She turns to look at me over her shoulder. "Yep, young hottie is *hot*!" Her free hand fans her face.

I swat at her shoulder.

"Well…" She draws out while fiddling with the photo on her phone. "Officer Kirchner's definitely on the hot scale. You definitely need to call him."

"I can't."

"Why?" She sets her phone down, placing all of her attention on me.

"He's way too young for me." I state the obvious.

"How old is he?" she asks.

"I don't know," I admit.

"Then, how do you know you're too old?" she counters, placing air quotes around "too old."

"Hello! You've seen him. He's your age." Internally, I cringe at the thought of Stephen being Lidia's age.

"Age doesn't matter," she states. "Besides, it's fashionable to be a cougar."

"Thanks," I deadpan.

"The only thing that matters is how you feel," she offers. "Clearly, he's into you; he gave you his number. Go out to lunch or get a coffee with him. It might be fun."

A small smile slips upon my face at the thought, while fear laced with excitement pulses through my veins.

"So, you'll call him?" she encourages, full of hope.

I bite my lip.

"He's off today," she reminds me. "Text him. Chat with him for a bit. You can get to know him better, then go to lunch another day."

I squint, processing her words. He *is* off today. If I wait, I may text him while he's on the job. I don't want to distract him; his job is too important.

"I may text him later tonight," I hedge. "What do you want for dinner?"

"Actually," she draws out, picking up her cell phone, "a couple of us are grabbing dinner and hanging out. I hate to back out on our dinner, but..."

"Go out; have fun," I encourage. "You aren't in Des Moines often enough to see all of your friends."

She rises from the pool's edge, sliding my cell phone toward me. "Text him. You can spend the evening chatting back and forth. Text him once, and I will drop it."

I draw in a deep breath, open my cell phone, and text.

**Me: Can you chat?**
**Me: This is Sylvie.**

Giggling at my nervousness, Lidia teases, "Congrats, Mom. Now, you are in a text-lationship."

## Chapter Thirty-Three
# SYLVIE

I drop my cell on the concrete when a FaceTime call rings.

"Answer it!" Lidia squeals.

"Hello," I greet, cringing at my own face in the corner of the screen.

"Hey," Stephen greets, smirking. "I'm free to chat."

"I meant on text," I explain, smoothing my t-shirt, making sure the white fabric isn't wet from the pool. "I could have been in my pajamas with a facial mask on. You shouldn't just FaceTime a woman."

"And if you were, I would have loved seeing and learning that about you," he responds. "What are you doing right now?"

I shake my head at him. "I'm getting ready to eat dinner with my daughter."

I rise from the pool, heading for the house.

"No, she's not," Lidia hollers from behind me. Quickly,

she comes to my side. "I'm backing out on her dinner to see friends. So, she's free."

My wide eyes cause Stephen to laugh. It's a deep, masculine laugh, causing my belly to flip-flop and butterflies to flutter their wings inside it.

"Let's get dinner," he suggests as if it's just that easy. "Super casual. We could get takeout and take it to the park."

It's my turn to speak. I know it is. I have no idea what to say. *Could I do "super casual" takeout at the park? When he handed me his card, he suggested a drink or coffee, not dinner of any kind.*

"She'll do it," Lidia answers for me.

"Uh..." I'm speechless.

"I'm in your area," he admits. "I can pick you up."

I prepare to argue, but Lidia, peeking through the blinds at the front window, catches my attention. She mouths, "He's here," while her finger points to my driveway.

*Holy crap!* I wanted to suggest I'd meet him, so I'd have my own vehicle when I wanted to leave.

"Are you in the area or sitting outside my house? This seems very stalker-ish to me, Officer," I tease.

I shouldn't tease. I should worry a bit that he remembers where I live and drove over here. *If I didn't text, would he have stopped?*

"You caught me," he confesses. "I just left Fredrik's—I mean Officer Calderon's house—and since I was in this part of town, I thought I'd drive by your house." His face now serious, he continues, "I just couldn't help myself." He shrugs. "The fact that you texted made me pull over. It's not safe to text and drive, you know."

"Well, come inside," I prompt. "I don't want my neighborhood watch to call the police on your dark truck lurking on our street."

Lidia opens the front door, waving him in. I disconnect the call as I make my way to the front room. Mentally, I run through my clothes, hair, and makeup, although it's too late to change it.

He opts not to enter the house, remaining on the front step. "It's a beautiful evening. Let's grab a bite and find a park bench."

Wide, nervous smile upon my face, I nod. He gifts me with a smile so wide it reaches his dark eyes, framed with long curling lashes. The warmth in my belly soothes my nerves a bit. He's much too sexy.

"I'll follow you in my car," I declare. "Give me a second." I wave to him before walking to the kitchen to grab my purse.

I can't make out the words Lidia shares with Stephen before she closes and locks the front door. She hugs me, excitement exuding from every pore.

"Since he's a cop," she shares, "I won't worry that he's taking you to a secluded part of the park to kill you." She laughs. She actually laughs while a small part of me worries that I'm too trusting. "Stop," she orders. "He's a good guy. You'll be in public, never alone."

"Then, why did you put that thought into my head?" I swat at her.

"This is so exciting." She claps in front of her chest, giggling. "You have to text or call me afterwards. I want to hear all about it. My mom's going on her first date!" She continues to clap while I shake my head at her.

## Chapter Thirty-Four
# STEPHEN

I back my truck from her driveway, pulling along the side of the street to wait for her. *I hope she won't change her mind.* It seems like forever before her garage door lifts. *I bre*athe a sigh of relief as her SUV pulls from the driveway. I wave to her in my rear-view mirror, then realize we haven't decided on a restaurant. I leave my truck; I hop out running to approach her door.

"We didn't decide what to eat," I tell her.

"You decide. I'll just follow you," she states.

*Really? She'd really let me, almost a total stranger, choose her meal?*

"Are you in the mood for Mexican, burgers, chicken, or Chinese?" I ask for a hint.

"Mexican sounds good," she answers.

"Tasty Tacos is close," I offer, running through all the options between here and the park in my head.

"Perfect. I've never tried it," Sylvie admits. "Lead the way," she prompts.

---

"How have you lived in the Des Moines area for all of your life and avoided Tasty Tacos?" I ask, bending my legs under the picnic table.

"I just never wanted to," she explains. "I think it's the name; it's kitschy."

"Well, you've missed out," I state. "They're not your average tacos. They fry the flour tortilla for the shell. I bought you two; don't worry if you can't eat both of them."

She peeks into her white sack before she pulls the tray with the wrapped tacos out. I take my first bite, watching her eyes assess the food in front of her. She worries her lower lip as she positions the paper, revealing half her taco, then takes a bite.

My eyes scurry between her mouth as she chews and her eyes for her reaction. She nods her head, still chewing her first bite.

"Good," she mumbles, hand over her mouth.

Unlike her, I swallow my food before I speak. "Never judge a book by its cover," I tease.

"Tacos are my weakness," she confesses. "This could be very bad for me."

"How can tacos be bad?" I ask.

"It's close to my house and tastes so good," she explains before taking another bite. "Mmm..." she moans, mouth full.

I shake my head. *I love it. I love that she's being herself, eating carbs in front of me, and holding nothing back with her reactions. She's real unlike so many women I meet. She's comfortable in her own skin; not trying to impress me by being fake.*

## Chapter Thirty-Five
# SYLVIE

Pulling into my garage, I'm suddenly aware I don't recall the drive home; our conversations replayed in my head during the drive. My nerves were not as I expected. I marvel that I am already so comfortable with him. I answered his questions, and I didn't hold back like I often do in my sessions with Edith.

I open the door to the house and am greeted by the excited sounds of Bocephus and Hagrid in the laundry room. I place my purse on the counter then free them from their kennels.

"Let's go potty," I urge. "C'mon. Let's go outside."

I open the sliding door, and they sprint to the edge of the grass to quickly relieve themselves. I plop down on the step and watch.

Stephen is right, it's a beautiful evening. Hagrid takes a seat beside me to watch the puppy trot around and sniff everything. Try as he might, Hagrid just can't keep up with Bo's puppy energy.

*I guess I should text Lidia.*

**Me: I'm home & safe**
**Lidia: Details**
**Me: We ate, we walked, we talked**
**Lidia: Uh-huh. Not getting off that easy**
**Me: Ate Tasty Tacos (smiling emoji)**
**Lidia: And…**
**Me: Found a picnic table at Ewing Park**
**Lidia: And…**
**Me: I had fun, we talked, evening passed quick**
**Lidia: Plan date #2?**
**Me: We left it open**
**Lidia: Do you want date #2?**
**Me: I think so**
**Lidia: (clapping emoji, winking emoji)**
**Me: You having fun?**
**Lidia: Yep, got to go!**

I shake my head. She was adamant I text her as soon as I got home, but she's too busy to really chat.

"Oh, well." I cuddle Hagrid to my side. "You guys will keep me company, won't you?" I rub his belly.

Of course, Bo sees me rubbing his friend and wobbles over for his turn. I pick him up, and we head inside. I plop on the sofa, Bo on my lap and Hagrid at my side. I use one hand on each of them, scratching their bellies and heads.

*Buzz.* My cell phone vibrates on the cushion beside us.

**Stephen: I had fun tonight**

Ahhh. He texted instead of waiting a day or two to call or ghost me.

**Stephen: What are you doing?**
**Me: Rubbing bellies**
**Stephen: Sounds kinky**
**Me: Hagrid & Bocephus don't think so**
**Stephen: 2 men. You're talented**
**Me: 2 men, 8 legs, 2 tails**
**Stephen: Ah. Your dogs**
**Me: Yes, what else?**
**Stephen: Plead the 5<sup>th</sup>**
**Me: What are you doing?**
**Stephen: Watching Die Hard for the millionth time**
**Me: I love that Christmas movie**
**Stephen: Excuse me? I think I misread that**
**Me: It's a Christmas movie**

I stare at my phone for several long moments. *Did I offend him, or did something come up?* I was only teasing. Well, sort of teasing.

"Hello," I greet, a wide smile upon my face, when a FaceTime call comes in.

"What part of *Die Hard* is a Christmas movie?" His head tilts to the side, and his brow furrows.

"The office Christmas party is the main scene." I remind him of something he knows if he's seen the movie more than once. "The entire movie takes place on Christmas Eve."

"*Die Hard* is *not* a Christmas movie," he argues.

## Chapter Thirty-Six
# SYLVIE

Days later, I glance over my shoulder. Riley sits in her highchair, playing with a little police car. She loves pushing the button and listening to the siren. I turn back to my griddle, flipping the grilled cheese. It needs a few more minutes to toast.

*Ding dong.* The doorbell rings. I quickly pull the skillet off the hot burner before heading for the door.

"Who could that be?" I ask Riley. She smiles at my words.

Through the peephole, I find Stephen on my front step. I open the door, signaling for him to come on in. He's in uniform, on duty today. We've chatted three times since our park dinner. I should find it odd that he randomly shows at my house, but I don't.

"Well, this is a surprise," I state, tending to the grilled cheese again. "Is this an official visit?"

"Fredrik had an appointment, so he dropped me off for

lunch. Mind keeping me company for 30 minutes?" Stephen asks. "Who's this?" He notices my little guest in her chair.

"This is Riley," I answer, keeping my attention on my work. "My neighbor, Dawn, had a committee meeting, so I offered to keep Riley for her."

"I like your car," he says to her.

She launches it onto the kitchen floor, claps, and giggles. She points at it saying, "Po."

"That's how she says, 'Police.'" I point to Stephen and say, "Police."

Riley points at Stephen. "Po."

I laugh as I turn my attention back to the grilled cheese. I place one on a saucer, then I make two more sandwiches, placing them in the skillet. I cut the cooling sandwich into tiny pieces and sit it on the tray for Riley.

"I love grilled cheese," Stephen claims.

"Good because that's all that's on the menu today," I tease.

Riley holds a bite out for him. When Stephen chews it, he makes a huge production of loving it. She claps happily. Then, he feeds her a bite. I plate our grilled cheese, add a pickle, and grab a bag of chips before placing them on the island.

## Chapter Thirty-Seven
## STEPHEN

The long afternoon and my shift finally end; I hurry through my shower and quickly dress. I don't want to waste any more time before I call Sylvie. Sitting in my recliner, I select her name then press call.

"Hey," Sylvie's disembodied voice greets.

"Am I looking at the ceiling or carpet?" I ask, turning my head in an effort to make out the video screen.

"It's a towel," she chuckles. "Give me a minute."

That sparks my attention; there are many possible scenarios involving a towel. Perhaps she's stepping out of the pool or, better yet, the shower. Thoughts of water droplets on her naked skin stir my cock to life. It's a good thing she'll only see from the chest up as we chat tonight. In my fantasy, I clutch the towel in both hands, caressing her everywhere with the pretense of drying her off.

"Earth to Stephen," Sylvie calls.

"Sorry." I scramble to focus on our call, leaving the fantasies for later.

I watch as she carries her phone from her kitchen onto the patio.

"Did I call at a bad time?" I ask.

"Nope," she states. "I finished my painting, so I'm done for the night. I was washing my hands when you called."

Thus, the towel. I prefer the thought of her in the shower. I clear my throat and attempt to clear my mind as well.

"Will I get to see the painting?" I love the sparkle my question sparks in her hazel eyes.

She purses her lips to the side. "Sharing ..." She stammers. "I'm not accustomed to sharing my pieces."

"C'mon," I nudge. "I'm no expert, just very interested in your work."

"We'll see," she answers. Her hand cups the back of her long, slender neck. "What's for dinner?"

"Honestly, I haven't thought of it," I confess, my mind solely focused on talking to her. "I'm not an expert at grilled cheese like you are."

A wide smile slides upon her lips. "You surprised me."

Squinting my eyes, I attempt to decipher her expression. It seems she liked my impromptu visit.

"I probably should have called, but I didn't want to give you the chance to make up an excuse," I explain.

"I..." she stutters. "I..."

"I took a chance, hoping you wouldn't make me sit on your porch until my partner returned," I tease.

"I thought about it," she deadpans. "But what kind of citizen would I be if I didn't provide lunch for a boy in blue?"

I chuckle.

"Next time, give me a heads up, and I'll prepare something more enticing than a grilled cheese sandwich," she states.

*So, she wants there to be a next time. She's inviting me to stop by on future lunch breaks. Nice.*

"You're good with kids," Sylvie states.

*Fuck! Here it comes.* Discussing this could end the good thing we have before it even starts. *Why'd she have to choose this topic?*

"I have six nieces and nephews," I inform her.

"You look intimidating in your uniform, but you melted to putty in Riley's hands when she smiled," Sylvie teases, her fingers pinching her lip at the corner of her mouth.

"I have a way with the ladies." I wink, attempting to make light of this topic.

Sylvie rises from her seat on the patio, calling for Bo and Hagrid to follow her into the house. I'm silent as the background shows her walk through the kitchen to sit on her sofa. She lays the phone down, and in the distance, I hear her talking to the dogs.

"You're quite a catch. Why haven't you settled down and started a family?" she asks.

*There it is.* The big question. "I love kids. Maybe it's because I'm a big kid myself."

"You'll make a great dad someday." Her statement hangs heavily in the night air.

"I guess I would..." I mumble, my mind scrambling for a way to change the subject or take the focus off of me. "Why didn't you have another?" I ask her.

After a long pause, Sylvie shares, "I wasn't ready for Lidia.

I had a long list of things I planned to do." Her eyes shift to the side as she bites her lips uncomfortably. "Don't get me wrong. I planned to have children, but not until my early 30s. When I took the pregnancy test, I cried for hours."

She looks to me for my reaction. "I mourned the life I hoped for. Morning sickness haunted me all day, and for the first three months, I rarely left the house. That's when my life changed." She shakes her head. "I focused all of my energy on Omar, Lidia, and our home. There wasn't time for anything else. I gave up all hope of following my dreams."

She sighs before continuing. "I knew there was no way I could handle a second child. I may have been greedy for thinking it, but I drew my line in the sand."

"How were you greedy?" I interrupt. "You gave them 100 percent; you gave them everything. That's not greedy—it's selfless." I then take in a deep breath.

"I'm the greedy one. I like my life. I have expensive toys and a job I love. I enjoy every minute I spend with my nieces and nephews. It's just... I can't... I couldn't..." Now, it's my turn to be uncertain of her reaction to my confession.

"I couldn't continue in law enforcement with a family. I couldn't bear the thought of my children worrying that I might not come home from work."

Sylvie jumps in. "There is a risk every day for everyone. Any profession has a risk for a car wreck, natural disaster, random gunman, or infectious diseases; the list is long."

"Yeah, but it's less random for officers. We put ourselves at risk every traffic stop and domestic disturbance call. Don't get me wrong; I love what I do. And to continue loving it, I can't have children," My eyes lock on hers. "So..." I draw out,

"I got a vasectomy. I may be greedy, but I won't let my love of career cause stress or pain to a child."

Sylvie nods. It's not the response I expected from her.

"You seem to know exactly what you want. If that means you want to remain single, that's your prerogative," she states, a small smile upon her lips.

*Hmm. She champions my thoughts.*

"Childless, yes," I agree. "Single? I'm just keeping things simple for now."

She squints her eyes at me, worrying her lower lip. My eyes lock on it, glistening in the light. I long to run my thumb over it before sucking on it.

*Focus, idiot. What were we talking about? Oh, yeah. Kids.*

"Kids can't fully understand the dangers and reasons I chose this job. A woman, the right woman..." I secretly hope she's the right woman. I have a feeling—intuition, maybe. There's something about her that causes me to hope for the first time that Sylvie is the right woman for me. "The right woman can weigh the pros and cons and choose whether or not I'm worth it."

"You're definitely worth it," she immediately responds. "The pros far outweigh the cons."

I tip my head to the side. She didn't hesitate; she didn't... She barely knows me, yet she believes the pros outweigh the cons. She likes me. I should ask her out on a real date. *Hmm... I can't rush her, and I need to plan.*

"I've never shared all this with anyone; not even my family knows," I admit in a whisper.

"I'm honored you shared with me, and I'll keep your secret," she promises.

"I did the same thing," she states. "I had a tubal ligation after Lidia was born. I wanted to ensure I wouldn't have more children." She chuckles hollowly, "I guess we were both greedy in that way."

## Chapter Thirty-Eight
# SYLVIE

Snacks and beverages border the patio, while pool toys and towels line the pool's edge. Mother Nature blessed us with a beautiful early-August Saturday. Umbrellas at the patio tables will provide shade from the bright sun. I select a local radio station and set a volume we can easily carry-on conversations over.

"Yoo-hoo..." Dawn calls beyond my privacy fence.

I unlock the gate, prop it open, and motion for my neighbor and new friend to come on in.

"You're the first to arrive," I greet.

"What can I do to help you set up?" she asks, following me through the patio door and into the house.

"I think it's all set up," I state, glancing around the kitchen.

"Perfect. Then, let's fix a drink and relax until other neighbors arrive," she suggests. "What shall we have?"

"Water, lemonade, beer, wine, or margaritas," I list.

"Margaritas it is!" Dawn cheers.

Again, I marvel at her vim and vigor. If I could bottle it up, I'd be a millionaire many times over. *Wait. I am a millionaire.* I don't feel like one. I'm not sure the reality will ever set in. I shake away those thoughts.

Dawn selects two glasses from the counter and wets then dips them in salt while I mix ingredients in the blender.

"We make a great team," Dawn smiles, holding her full glass toward mine.

We clink our rims and take a long sip.

"Mmm," Dawn moans. "You have no idea how much I needed this today."

"Where's Riley?" I ask, just now realizing she's not in her arms or stroller nearby.

"A playdate with my best friend's granddaughter," she states between sips.

"You're lucky to have a friend with a child the same age."

"You're telling me," she agrees. "When my sons watch Riley, I worry the entire time I'm away. When she's on a playdate, I can relax."

The doorbell rings.

"Crud. I forgot to hang my sign." I return my glass to the counter then grab the tape and sign from the kitchen island. "It instructs guests to use the side gate to enter the pool area," I inform her as I walk to the door.

Dawn follows me to the front door. She introduces me to the couple that live down the street before she urges them to follow her around the side of the house. I hang my sign then scurry through the house to meet my guests poolside.

The party's perfect. While some neighbors visit under the shade of the umbrellas, others dangle their feet in the water or swim with the children. This was a great way for me to break the ice and meet my neighbors.

My brow furrows as loud voices draw our attention to the open gate. It's Lidia. She said she couldn't make it, yet she stands in front of us now.

"The party can start now. I'm here!" she shouts, her arms above her head.

"I thought you couldn't come," I greet as I approach her.

"We moved study group to tomorrow evening," she informs, lowering her large bag to the stone patio.

"Let me introduce you to everyone." I motion for her to walk with me toward the crowd. "If I can have your attention," I call to my guests. "This is my daughter, Lidia. She attends college in Iowa City."

The crowd smiles, waves, and cheers, "Go Hawkeyes!"

Lidia's classmate slips through the gate to join us, and my nerves spike. When Lidia told me she couldn't come, I invited Stephen to bring a couple of friends.

*Lidia will spend time with Stephen.* Although she's been here during a phone call, I'm nervous about them spending time together.

"Psst," Dawn seeks my attention. "What's wrong?"

I shake my head.

"Let's go make another pitcher of margaritas," she prompts, locking her elbow with mine and pulling me inside. "Spill it."

"It's nothing really," I state.

"Nope. Not buying it," she orders.

"Lidia wasn't coming. She said she had a study group," I inform my friend. "She caught me off guard," I lie.

Dawn's furrowed brow and squinting eyes inform me she knows there's more to it. Thankfully, she lets it go for now.

## Chapter Thirty-Nine
# SYLVIE

Later, my phone in my back pocket signals I have a text.

**Stephen: We're here**

My heart pounds hard against my ribcage as butterflies flutter in my stomach. Looking up from my phone, my eyes meet Lidia's.

"What's up?" she inquires.

"Um," I stammer. "So, I neglected to tell you... I invited Stephen to bring a couple of friends to the party."

"Cool," she grins.

"He's here." I extend my cell phone, showing her the text. "Um, can we not make a big deal about it in front of everyone?"

"Phish." Lidia swats my shoulder. "No one will even notice."

I follow my daughter into the house, through the kitchen, and toward the front door.

Lidia answers the door when they approach. "Hi. C'mon in." She swings the door wide, leaning on it.

"Hi, guys," I greet. "Head straight on back to the pool."

Lidia raises an eyebrow at me after all three men pass. "His photo didn't do him justice. He is so..." she draws out the word, "good looking."

"Shh," I admonish as they are only a few feet ahead of us.

She mouths, "Wow," before we step onto the patio.

Stephen turns to face us. "Guys, this is Sylvie and Lidia."

The guys smile and wave.

"Make yourselves at home," I urge nervously, pointing out areas of the backyard. "The coolers are full, the bathroom is in the pool shed, and snacks are already on the table. If you need anything else, don't hesitate to ask."

Stephen's friends move towards the snack table to drop off their towels and shoes, giving us a moment of privacy while surrounded by many of my neighbors.

"I know you've briefly talked on the phone," my voice breaks, exposing my nerves, "but Stephen, this is my daughter, Lidia."

He extends his arm to shake her hand, stating, "This isn't awkward at all, right?"

The two laugh as I nervously scan the crowd.

"I hope you're ready," Lidia says with hands on her hips. "Now that I know you are seeing my mom, I've got you under my microscope." She attempts to remain serious but cracks up and laughter escapes.

Stephen blows out the breath he was holding in relief. Lidia encourages her friend to join Stephen's friends near the snacks to make introductions.

---

As the sun sets, the neighbors say their goodbyes. One by one, they leave; my backyard grows quiet. Dawn helps me wash the wine and margarita glasses before she excuses herself to pick up Riley.

Alone in the house, I duck into the powder room and splash cold water on my neck. With hands on the counter, I stare at my reflection. The pink upon my nose hints at hours in the afternoon sun. I didn't reapply sunscreen.

"Mom?" Lidia's voice calls from the kitchen. "Need any help?"

I scurry from the restroom, smiling at my daughter who is dripping wet just outside the patio door. Shaking my head, I emerge from the house to face Stephen and his friends.

---

"Wait a minute," one of Stephen's buddies demands. "How young were you when you had Lidia?"

The other friend and Stephen swat him in the back of the head.

"First, you never—and I mean never—ask a woman her age," Stephen lectures.

"And dude, it's none of your business," Lidia adds. "Just know she was in her 20s and leave it at that."

"I didn't mean it in a bad way," Stephen's friend defends.

"She looks more like Lidia's sister than her mother. I meant it as a compliment."

I pull Stephen closer to where I sit on the edge of the pool. "This is the whole reason I invited you to the barbecue," I remind him. "We want everyone to meet and get our age difference out in the open." When I smile in Stephen's direction, his eyes glue on my mouth. "His comments don't bother me," I promise.

## Chapter Forty
# SYLVIE

"Lidia have a new boyfriend?" Dawn asks as she walks to her mailbox the next day.

My garden-gloved hands pause. I sit back on my calves and look her way, raising one hand to block the bright sun. "What?" I ask, not understanding her question.

With mail in hand, she walks towards me at the front flower bed.

"I've seen a young man in a dark pickup visiting your house, and he was at the pool party," Dawn explains. "I figured he was Lidia's new fella. I guess I missed the chance to set her up with one of my sons."

"Lidia prohibits me setting her up," I inform her.

"From what I've seen, she's hooked herself a handsome young man," Dawn continues.

I rise, pulling off my dirty gloves. "He's not Lidia's boyfriend." I answer her initial question.

"Oh, I saw them chatting at your pool party." Dawn purses her lips to one side. "Is he doing work on the house?"

"Um..." I hedge, not knowing what to say. The truth is all I can think of. "He's here to spend time with me."

*There. It's out. Public. Now, for her reaction.*

"I see," Dawn says, her face morphing into a wide smile. "I've chilled a bottle of wine. Why don't you lose those gloves and come enjoy it with me?"

*She'll probably follow me inside if I attempt to evade her.* I toss my garden gloves to the sidewalk and follow her into her house. *This won't be bad. She's not my mother. She's my age. I hope she won't judge me.*

"Where's Riley?" I ask, taking a stool at the kitchen counter.

"She's on a play date," Dawn states.

"Two days in a row. Aren't you lucky?" My nerves can be heard in my voice.

Filling my wine glass to the brim, she prompts, "Drink up."

"In a hurry or trying to get me drunk?" I ask.

"Both," she replies. "I want to know everything. How you met, all of his details, and..." She wiggles her eyebrows at me. "I mean *all* of the details."

I sip my wine, aware of her eyes glued to me. "Well, you're the reason we met," I confess.

"I am?" she questions.

"His name is Stephen Kirshner, and he's a police officer."

"Seriously?" she squeals, her brows high and mouth open wide.

I nod, sipping more wine.

"When you called in the noise complaint, two very handsome officers rang my doorbell," I share.

"Two?" she queries.

"Yes. The older one was a silver fox," I share. "That's how I described him to Lidia."

"And the young one?" Dawn presses, on the edge of her seat.

"He's a young hottie," I blush.

"I'd say he is," Dawn laughs. "I've only caught a few glimpses. He looks fine," she draws out.

We drink wine for a few quiet moments.

"So, he's a cop." Dawn urges me to continue.

"Yeah. I met him and his partner the night you turned me in. A few weeks later, I bumped into the two of them working at Zoo Brew," I divulge. "Then, get this: the two were working at a bike night I attended. I accused them of stalking me."

"Three times," she counts. "Three times you saw the two of them in uniform? You're so lucky." She fans her face.

*She must have an active imagination.*

"I love a man in uniform," she sighs. "So, did he hit on you while he was working?"

"No, not in uniform," I answer. "I bumped into the two of them shopping at Scheel's. Stephen was helping his partner's daughter shop."

Her lips pursed; Dawn's eyes implore me to continue.

"There's nothing to tell, really. He gave me his cell phone number." I shrug.

"He gave you his number and...?" she urges, hands prompting me to continue.

"Flustered, I called Lidia for advice," I share. "She

explained that since he gave me his number, he let me have control. He had no way to contact me."

"So, when did you call him?"

I sigh heavily. "Lidia urged me to reach out to him that day as I knew he was off work. Not wanting to distract him while he's on patrol, I texted him." I smile, remembering. "Instead of replying to my text, he video called me."

"Whoa..." Dawn's eyes are wide as is her smile.

"With Lidia's help, he coaxed me to follow him to Tasty Tacos then to a park to eat and chat." I shrug, lifting my wine glass to my lips.

Unable to wait for me to continue, Dawn speaks. "I'm not really a super nosey neighbor," she promises, index finger crossing her heart. "I happened to be out watering my plants when he pulled up once."

I wrinkle my nose at her.

"He's appeared in a few of my security camera videos," she further confesses, attempting to make light of this fact.

I tilt my head to the side, furrowing my brow. "Do your cameras point to my front yard?"

She pulls her lips into her mouth sheepishly. "In order to capture my side yard and the end of my driveway, I also see most of the street and yard in front of your house."

I'm not sure if I should feel safer knowing her cameras allow her to police part of my yard or be offended that she keeps track of my guests coming and going.

"I'm not a voyeur," she states. "My boys installed the cameras, worried for my safety." She shrugs, making light of it. "I get an alert on my phone when there is movement in the area."

"So, you know when I pull from my driveway and prune the plants in my front flower beds?"

"Yes, but I delete those as soon as I recognize Lidia and you," she vows. "I can't promise I won't happen to be out every time he triggers the cameras on his visits," Dawn giggles, waggling her eyebrows at me.

"You're horrible," I chuckle. My wine finished, I place the glass on the counter. "I'm not sure there should be a next time."

"Phish," she swats the air. "Have fun. At our age, we deserve it."

"That's just it," I inform her. "He's too young for me."

"Nonsense," she argues. "In junior high, a year's difference is normal. In high school, a year or two difference is acceptable." She pours more wine as she continues. "In college, up to five years difference seems appropriate. After age 25, anything goes."

I wonder if these rules are written somewhere. She recites them as if she's visited this topic often. I cringe. Perhaps she tells her sons this.

"So, by your rules," I tease, "I'm too old for your sons."

She swats at the air between us. "How old is Stephen?" she asks.

"Twenty-eight," I answer.

"My sons are only 21 and 24," Dawn states. "I don't believe you're too…"

"Stop!" I shout. "You would not want me dating your boys."

"Stephen's nearly 30," she reminds me. "I doubt he acts like a young, 20-something, going out partying."

"But we don't know," I state the obvious. "He could still

like to party and play with his expensive toys." I sip my wine, playing with the stem of my glass as I continue.

"Excuse me?" Dawn raises her voice. "You've only eaten fast food, walked in the park with him, and allowed him to swim in your pool."

*Why does the last point sound seedy?*

"That's too soon to make assumptions. You only have the facts to judge by." She leans forward in her seat towards me. "He's a cop. He probably likes to follow rules and laws since he's a cop. He showed he's okay with allowing you to lead when he gave you his number instead of asking for yours. And you mentioned he babysits for his partner's kids. All in all, he seems like an adult instead of a man-child. He's worth a date; you need to keep an open mind."

"It's a 14-year difference. Fourteen years is a *big* difference," I hedge, my voice rising in pitch.

"You certainly don't act your age," Dawn explains. "Thus, the 14 years shrinks. If he's a bit more mature for his age, it shrinks even further."

Her rationale seems strong. I find myself wanting to cling to it.

"Ahh..." She smiles, pointing to my forehead. "You're considering it," she cheers.

"I'll keep an open mind," I promise.

Dawn claps, bouncing in her seat like a child.

"I need to find you a man," I tell her.

"Uh-uh," she argues. "I have no time for a man. Riley is more than I can handle most of the time. There's a reason we have children when we're young and have energy." She shakes her head. "When she naps, I'm so tired I need to nap but also need to do the long list of things I can't do while she's awake. It's a constant battle. Do I rest then complete the tasks when she goes to bed at night or complete my tasks and be exhausted the remainder of the day?"

"I hope you know, I'm available to help with Riley. I can give you a couple of hours to catch up when you need to." I offer.

"Then, we will both be tired," Dawn quips, and we laugh.

## Chapter Forty-One
# STEPHEN

"So, tell me more about your family," Sylvie prompts.

I watch her play with the long ears of her Basset hound on my phone screen. I'm jealous; I long for her slender fingers to fondle me with her affection.

"I'm the youngest at 28. My parents are in their 70s. I have an older brother that's 48 and an older sister that's 42. I was a mistake." I smile, attempting to make light of the obvious age difference with my siblings.

Sylvie raises her eyebrows, urging me to continue.

"I have a nephew that's 23 years old; I'm not much older than him." I purse my lips to the side, shrugging.

"My mom claims I have an old soul. I tend to gravitate towards people older than me. Heck, Fredrik is my best friend, and the guys I hang with are all older than me."

My eyes move to her lips for a moment before I continue. "So, when I told my mother I met a woman, the first thing she asked me was, 'Is she older than you?'" I chuckle. "Now, I didn't share any more details about your age. I only told her how we kept bumping into each other and asked for her advice in planning our first date."

I sigh, a slight smile upon my face. "Of course, she shared all the details with my siblings, and they hound me incessantly for details about you. I'm still avoiding those questions."

"You could talk to them," Sylvie states. "Stop avoiding them; it's torture."

"If I do, all the bribes will end," I share. "They've bought me lunch a couple of times, my sister cleaned my apartment for me, and they even bring me casseroles and stuff."

"You're bad," she laughs.

"So, I'm supposed to invite you to a family barbecue two weeks from Thursday." My eyes peer deep into hers, awaiting her reaction. "Are you ready to meet my family? Or is it too soon? Remember, I'm new to relationships. If it's too soon, just tell me. It's no big deal, really," I blabber.

"It's not too soon. It's..." She struggles to express the reason for her hesitation. "I think we need to discuss what we are before we..."

"Okay," I drawl out. "You are my girlfriend."

Sylvie beams, causing my body to grow hot.

"I am?" she teases. "And what does being your girlfriend mean to you?"

"Exclusive, becoming best friends, and ..." I waggle my eyebrows suggestively.

She laughs at my insinuation.

"What do *you* think we are?" I toss her question back at her.

"Honestly, even with all of my research, I'm still not sure

how the dating scene works now. I have tons of fun chatting with you. I'm exclusively yours." She pauses, her eyes scanning my face through the phone screen. "I wasn't sure if you were on the same page."

I long to pull her tightly against me, peppering kisses on every inch of her. As much as I look forward to our video calls, I'd rather be with her.

"Will you be my girlfriend?"

"What's in it for me?" She giggles, her cheeks pinking.

---

## Sylvie

"He told me I'm officially his girlfriend," I state.

Lidia coughs. "What was your answer?"

I smile like a middle school girl, maybe even blush a bit. "I'm his girlfriend."

"That's so cool," she cheers, hopping up and down, clapping.

"What is?" I ask.

"My mom has a boyfriend that makes her smile nonstop." Lidia pauses to inhale. "I've worried about you alone in Des Moines. Now, when we talk, you have stories to tell me about during your phone calls. I can hear happiness in your voice over the phone. He's good for you. And he makes me feel less guilty for being in Iowa City," Lidia confesses.

"I'm not alone; you have no need to worry," I promise. "I do spend time with Dawn and Riley, and I have a few committee meetings coming up in the next couple of weeks. So, I'm not alone."

## Chapter Forty-Two
# SYLVIE

The next evening, my cell rings. I quickly wipe my hands on my apron before answering.

"Hello," I greet.

"Sylvie, this is Nelson, Dawn's son. I'm watching Riley, and I need your help."

"What's up?" I ask, noting Riley whaling in the background.

"I'm babysitting while Mom's at the JDRF Gala tonight." I hear worry in his masculine voice. "She's teething, running a fever, and I can't find any children's medicine. I've tried everything."

"I'm on my way," I state, slipping on shoes.

I quickly walk to my neighbor's door while removing my apron from around my waist. I find the door open with Nelson holding a fussy Riley in his arms.

"Can you hold her for a while?" Nelson pleads. "I need a bathroom break."

He passes Riley to me then darts down the hallway. I hug little Riley, placing a kiss on her forehead.

"It's okay," I coo. "I know it hurts, but we'll fix that. I promise."

I continue baby talking as I rummage through the kitchen drawers and cabinets. Next, I dig through Riley's diaper bag on the dining room table. I find a bottle of children's Tylenol; to my dismay, it's empty. I lay it on the tabletop and continue digging through the bag. Next, I search the nursery with no luck.

Nelson returns with out-stretched arms, and I pass Riley back to him.

"I've looked everywhere," I state. "All I found was this empty bottle."

"Would you mind driving to the store to get some?" he asks.

"Sure," I respond. "Anything else you need?"

"Nope," he answers, handing me a set of keys. "Take my truck."

"No, I'll take mine," I reply.

"I insist," Nelson argues, forcing his keys into my palm.

I take the proffered keys and head for the door. I don't like to drive strange vehicles. I know from my talks with Dawn that his truck is new, and he's very careful with it. Although I have the strong urge to take my SUV when I get my purse from my house, I abide by his wish and take his truck.

I must hop and pull myself inside the big truck with the handle mounted inside the door. I place his key fob in the exterior pocket of my purse, start the mammoth beast, and nervously pull from the driveway.

I feel I'm a long way above the road. Other cars cower in comparison when I pass. At the closest grocery store, I park at the far end of a row of parked cars as I remember Dawn telling me he usually takes up two parking spots to prevent door dings. My conscience won't let me take up two parking spots, so I park farther down in hopes of no one parking beside me.

I dart inside, pick up some Orajel and children's Tylenol, pay the cashier, and dart toward the end of the lot. I toss the sack into the truck before I climb up into the driver's seat.

When I pull from the parking lot, I notice the check engine light is on. *Crap! Nelson's going to kill me if I broke his new truck.* I quickly look for other warning lights on the dash. It doesn't appear to be overheating, so I carefully watch the dummy lights as I drive back.

Walking to Dawn's door, I realize I left the grocery bag in the truck, and I jog back to fetch it. My nerves increase as I'll have to tell Nelson about the truck.

Back inside the house, I rub Orajel on Riley's upper and lower gums. Nelson holds her tight in his arms as I use the dropper with the children's Tylenol. The two actions upset her further.

"Let me hold her for a while," I offer, my arms outstretched. "She loves my dogs. Want to come over to my house until she calms?"

Nelson nods, and I open the front door. The sight of his truck reminds me to tell him about the warning light.

"On my way home," I begin, hesitant, "your check engine light came on."

"Huh?" he asks, brow furrowed.

"Just the one light," I promise.

He joins me on the front step.

"Sylvie, that's not my truck," Nelson states calmly. "Tonight's not the night to be pulling tricks on me."

"It's no trick," I state. "And the check engine light stayed on the entire ride home."

Nelson opens the driver's door then looks back to me, his worried face lit by the interior light of the truck.

"What do you mean it's not your truck?" I'm confused.

He reaches in then dangles another set of keys in front of me. Even in the little light from the truck, I know they are not the set he handed me earlier. I quickly approach the truck.

"This is not my truck," Nelson slowly says. "You have to take it back before someone reports it stolen."

*Stolen. I stole a truck. Fuck!* Bile climbs my throat. I have to get back to the store before the police are involved.

"Take Riley to my house," I instruct. "Play with the dogs until she calms down. After that, she'll probably fall asleep."

I lift myself into the stranger's truck. "I'll call you to let you know what happens at the store."

## Chapter Forty-Three
# SYLVIE

As I pull into the grocery parking lot, I see a police car in the area I previously parked Nelson's truck. They stand at the back of his truck with an older couple. I pull in next to them.

As I hop out, I quickly explain with my hands held up, "It was an accident. See? I have the keys. I just took the wrong truck."

When I join the group behind Nelson's truck, everyone looks at me.

"You see?" I explain further. "It's my friend's new truck. I didn't want to drive it, but he insisted. I parked it way out here because he's paranoid about door dings. I ran inside to get supplies for a teething baby. When I came out, I climbed in the truck where I parked. I didn't see there were two trucks parked here." I pause for a quick breath.

"I assumed the key fob in my purse unlocked the door and allowed me to start the truck. When I told my friend his check engine light was on, he went to check and told me it wasn't his truck. I didn't mean to steal it." My eyes beg them to believe my story.

I hear a familiar, deep laugh behind me. I don't turn around. *This is just my luck.* Officer Kirchner and Officer Calderon join the group. Part of me is glad he is here; he'll believe I didn't mean to steal a truck. Another part of me knows he will tease me about this.

"I'm not pressing charges," the man standing by the other officers states. "We left our keys inside, and this wouldn't have happened if we'd locked it."

I smile at the man and his wife. "I'm so sorry. I should have paid closer attention."

"No worries, dear," the woman promises, patting my forearm.

"I'm not filing paperwork on this one," one officer states.

"I wouldn't even know how to start paperwork on this one," another officer teases.

When the two officers retreat to their patrol car, I'm left standing with Officer Calderon and Officer Kirchner. Both smirk at me.

"This can't be the first time this has happened," I offer in my defense.

"I've never seen it," Officer Calderon states, fighting a grin.

"You really didn't know it was a different truck?" Stephen queries.

"I was in a hurry to get Riley's medicine. She's very fussy," I share. "I knew it was a dark truck with dark interior."

"You really need to pay closer attention to details and

your surroundings," Stephen offers, shaking his head, arms crossed over his broad chest.

"It's over now. Everyone has the right truck, and no one was hurt," I defend.

"It's not going to be over for a long, long time," Stephen's partner laughs.

"How long will the teasing on this one last?" I ask, hands on my hips.

Stephen laughs, "There will be no expiration date on this one."

## Chapter Forty-Four
# SYLVIE

"I got your text," Dawn explains when I open my front door.

"Nelson needed a break," I share. "I hope you don't mind that I kept her over here for a couple hours."

"Of course not," Dawn smiles. "I'm upset with myself. I had the teething meds in the backseat of my car. I meant to leave them with Nelson."

"She's fine now; no worries," I promise.

"I'll have one of those," Dawn says, motioning to my wine glass. "While we drink, you can tell me what happened tonight," she states. "Nelson said you were hilarious."

"Odd." I pull out a wine glass. "He didn't find it funny at the moment."

"So…?" she prompts.

We settle into comfortable spots on my sectional sofa with wine glasses in hand and dogs curled up near us on the floor.

"Well, you know I went to the store to get teething

supplies," I start. "Nelson insisted that I drive his truck. I tried to argue, but he wouldn't have it." I shrug. "So, I drove his truck and parked at the far end of the parking lot. I remembered what you said about his paranoia of door dings." I smile at Dawn. "I shopped then hurried back home," I continue.

"What's the funny part?" Dawn prompts.

"I suggested that we bring Riley to my house. I planned to let her play with the dogs while the medicine kicked in for her to sleep," I share.

"On my way home from the store, the check engine light came on in the truck. I remembered to tell Nelson as we headed for my house. Of course, when I told him, he immediately went to check on his truck." I take a sip of wine before this next part.

"When he got closer, he told me it wasn't his truck. He opened the driver's door and stated again that it was not his truck," I explain.

"But it was his truck, right?" Dawn asks.

I shake my head. "It was *not* his truck."

"How?" she asks, confused.

"He took Riley to my place, and I went back to the store," I explain. "The police were called and standing with a couple by Nelson's truck when I pulled back into the parking lot."

She's not laughing. Maybe she won't see this as funny.

"I explained that I was in a hurry and that I had driven my neighbor's truck. I assumed the key fob in my purse unlocked it and allowed me to drive it. The other couple left theirs unlocked with the keys in it. I didn't pay attention that there were two dark trucks parked there, and..."

"Oh. My. Gosh. You stole a truck!" Dawn blurts.

We both look to Riley who is sleeping on the floor. She doesn't even flinch at Dawn's loud voice.

"I didn't steal it. I mistakenly borrowed it," I argue. "And I returned it immediately."

"I wish I could have seen Nelson's face when he found out it wasn't his truck," she laughs.

"It was too dark to really see, but in the dome light of the truck I could see he was mad," I share.

Dawn's still laughing. I love her laugh; it's contagious. I join her in laughter. We laugh so hard, we have to place our wine glasses on the table.

"My side hurts," I say through my laughter, holding my side.

Dawn snorts. This causes both of us to laugh harder.

"I haven't.... have more..." I can't continue to talk through my laughter. I attempt to breathe in long breaths as I wipe the tears from my eyes.

Dawn joins me in taking deep breaths but loses her battle and continues to laugh.

"Stephen was on the scene," I sputter.

Leaning forward in laughter, Dawn tumbles to the floor. She rolls into a ball on her side, laughing. She knows he teases me; this will give him new fodder.

I move onto the floor beside my friend. Still laughing, I smile back at her. Slowly, her laughter turns to giggles. I'm not sure how long we lay on my floor, but I enjoy every minute of it.

## Chapter Forty-Five
# SYLVIE

Dawn and I stand in the water up to our waist, trying to remain cool on a hot, sunny Friday afternoon. Riley laughs, slapping the water around her pool float. Occasionally, we push her back and forth between us.

"I have a personal problem," I blurt, unsure how to bring up this topic.

"Do tell," Dawn encourages.

"I shaved my bikini area," I begin. "Now, it's growing back in, and it itches something fierce."

Dawn's deep belly laugh elicits a snort. She slaps her hand over her mouth, and I join her giggles.

"I shouldn't be laughing," I tell her. "It *really* itches."

I turn all of my attention toward Riley while Dawn collects herself.

"Why would you shave?" she asks.

"I read on the internet that it's popular now," I inform

my new friend. "They make it sound like guys expect it from the women they date."

"You should stick to older men," Dawn states. "Guys our age aren't picky."

I stare wide-eyed at her. She's my friend; I expected this from a stranger, but she seemed supportive.

She raises her arms, palms toward me. "I'm kidding." One of her hands begins rubbing my upper arm. "I'm sorry. I was trying to be funny. I think it's awesome." She pulls Riley along beside her as she wades towards the steps. "You should wax. That way, you don't have razor burn and itching."

"I read about that, too," I explain. "It's got to hurt something fierce; don't you think?"

"It's ten minutes of pain for four to six weeks without shaving daily. If you can survive childbirth, you can handle waxing in that area." Dawn tilts her head, waiting for my response. "My salon offers waxing services."

"I need to think about it," I admit, wading toward the stairs. "You can text me your salon's information."

I'm unsure if grooming my bikini area is part of my new life, but I might give it a try.

## Chapter Forty-Six
# SYLVIE

So, here I am, nervously playing with a cocktail napkin at the corner of the bar with a perfect line of sight to the little stage.

I saw a flyer at the music store, back when taking my guitar lessons, and after my YouTube channel blew up, Edith encouraged me to challenge myself with a live performance.

Bongo, the bartender, returns with my first beer.

"You're new," he states. "I'd remember if I had seen you in here before."

I claim to have just moved into town. It's true; I moved from Norwalk to Des Moines. He doesn't need to know I moved less than 10 miles. He slides my Bud Light draught on the napkin closer to me then returns to the other patrons.

The night quickly passes; I'm on my second beer at the end of the first band's performance. I watch as the next group of gangly, high school boys nervously tune instruments, arms barely strong enough to hold their guitars and basses. I can't stifle my giggle.

"What's so funny?" Bongo asks.

I share, and he chuckles.

"I promise the two after this one are great bands that perform here often." He smiles before taking more orders.

While watching this band, a large, bulky guy squeezes between my barstool and the next. I keep my focus on the stage. In my periphery, I see him hold on up two fingers while ordering and taps the bar near my empty mug.

"Another?" his deep voice growls near my ear.

I nod as my skin prickles.

"You've got to be kidding me," he says when I turn to face him. "Now, I wonder if you are stalking me." He looks offended.

"I was here first," I defend before calling out, "Bongo, who got here first? Him or me?" I point my thumb at each of us.

Pleading the fifth, the bartender raises his palms up and retreats.

"If I recall, this was the type of music playing through my speakers when you banged on my door," I state.

Smirking, he gives in. "I haven't noticed you here before."

"Seriously? You keep track?" I scoff. "You're the second person to comment that it's my first time here."

"We pay attention when hot women are involved," he states.

*Hot women? He thinks I'm hot? Easy. Play it cool. Pull it together, woman.*

"So, how often are you here?" I ask.

"I come every now and then when I'm working day shift. Much less often when I'm on nights," he admits.

"Oh." I chug from my ice-cold mug.

He watches, brow furrowed.

Not wanting to alarm Officer Kirshner, I explain, "I'm using Uber tonight. I'm ready for a night out, and none of my friends enjoy my taste in music." *Especially not my daughter.* I keep that thought to myself. "I'll be using Uber as my designated driver."

---

"Last call. Last call for alcohol," Bongo yells, after ringing the loud metal bell mounted behind the bar.

Stephen orders a drink for each of us.

"I'm using Uber, too," he declares, clanking his bottle to my mug before we each take a drink. "I think we should go out next Thursday night," he announces, catching me by surprise.

"You do? That's interesting." I smirk in his direction. "I happen to have plans for Thursday."

"So, cancel them." He graces me with his sexy, crooked grin.

"I don't want to," I coyly reply. "Maybe..."

"Yeah?" he eagerly prompts, a glimmer of home in his brown eyes.

"Maybe you could go with me," I state, eyes scanning his entire face.

"Go where?"

"I have two tickets to the Communicable concert Thursday night at the State Fair," I boast.

He spews the drink he just took, causing me to snort.

"That's hilarious," he says.

Confused, I tilt my head with a furrowed brow. "I don't think it's hilarious."

"Well, that's because you don't know the punch line," he states.

I raise an eyebrow, urging him to explain.

"I hoped to take you to the State Fair on Thursday," he confesses.

Now, I chuckle. "Let me see if I have this straight. You'll get me into the fair, and I'll get you into the concert."

"It's a date," he states.

"I haven't said yes yet," I tease.

"But you will." He leans closer, our noses now an inch apart. "Won't you?"

I nod.

He sighs. "Finish your beer, and we'll share an Uber," he insists.

*Bossy much?*

---

At my house, I pause nervously before opening the car door. "I'd offer to let you come in, but all the beer makes me very, very sleepy," I admit.

"If you offered, I'd have declined gently," he promises, smiling.

*Ahh...* He is so sweet and definitely too good to be true.

## Chapter Forty-Seven
# SYLVIE

The next week, I'm crossed-legged on Edith's couch, fiddling with the tip of my shoelaces.

"I've been asked out on a date," I blurt.

"How did you feel when he asked you?" Edith counters. "And did you accept?"

*How did I feel? Hmm...*

Sensing my hesitation, Edith tries a different route. "How'd the two of you meet?"

"Oddly enough, we've bumped into each other several times." I answer honestly. "Do you believe in signs?"

Edith quirks her head to one side. "Explain what you mean by signs."

"He asked me to go to the State Fair with him on Thursday for a date, and I just so happen to have two concert tickets and VIP passes for that night at the fair."

"Quite a coincidence," Edith smiles.

"That's only one of the times we bumped into each

other," I sigh, preparing to spill my guts. "He was one of the cops that came to my new home for the noise complaint. Then, I saw him at a Zoo Brew event *and* the Southside Bike Night."

"As if those weren't enough signs," I continue, "We were both shopping at the mall. That's when he slipped me his cell phone number."

"So, you called him?" Edith seeks more details.

"I texted him," I state. "He immediately video-phoned me."

"Did you answer?" she asks, no longer taking notes on her tablet.

I nod. "He was driving through my neighborhood and pulled over in front of my house to make the call." I shrug. "He doesn't text and drive," I explain.

Edith's face no longer looks amused; she's concerned.

"He's not a stalker," I quickly state. "Well, it's kind of a running joke between us. With each chance meeting, we accuse the other of being our stalker. He's a cop," I remind her. Again, I shrug. "When he bumped into me at the Brickhouse, he asked me on a second date."

Edith squints with her head tipped to the right.

"Second date? So, you went on a first date before the Brickhouse?" Her hands play with the stylus in her lap.

"No," I answer. "Yes." I bite my lip. "He claims we went on a first date; I don't agree."

Edith's head tilts to the left, eyes still assessing.

"So," I draw out as I attempt to explain, "when he video-called me, I gave in. I followed him to pick up fast food. Then, we went to a park to eat. Since we drove separately, I don't classify it as a date."

"How long were you at the park?" she pries.

"After we ate, we walked and talked," I share. "It was like an hour or two."

She smirks. Edith actually smirks at me. *Is that even professional?*

"You think it counts as a first date, don't you?" I query.

"It's not my place to tell you what to believe. I'm simply here to guide you," Edith states. "When he asked you on the second or first date, did you say yes?"

I nod, smiling.

"How do you feel?"

*Here we go again.* Time to uncover deeper feelings and put my fears into words.

"I'm too old to date, and he's much younger than me." I pause. When she doesn't jump in, I continue. "I gave in, though; I figure I shouldn't ignore all of the signs."

"What concerns do you have?" Edith continues her prying while jotting notes. "Do you foresee any issues arising during the date?"

"I'm worried how Lidia feels about me dating. I don't want her to think I've forgotten her father. And then, there's the whole age difference. It will be painfully obvious I'm a cougar."

"If the age difference concerns you, perhaps you should talk to him about it," she offers. "Does it matter what others think more than what the two of you think?"

I shake my head. Every visit, we discuss that my feelings matter more than what others think of me.

"I think it's a very public venue; that might make it an easier first date." I make eye contact for a moment before looking down at my hands in my lap. "But that also means more people will see the age difference..."

"Will you know all of them?" Edith butts in. "Will you ever see them again?"

I shake my head.

"Do their thoughts affect your happiness?" She continues to drive her point home.

When I shake my head again, she continues, "All that matters is the thoughts and feelings the 2 of you have. And your thoughts and feelings are the *most* important. You've worked hard to bring your feelings to the front instead of always putting others first and suppressing your own."

Nodding, I look up. "I chose the concert and splurged on the VIP access. In the past, I've heard about concerts of interest to me and did nothing more. I've missed many things of interest to me. By attending this concert, I'm embracing life—enjoying it. Thus, I'm putting my wants first."

## Chapter Forty-Eight
# SYLVIE

I have one more errand before I head home. I did my research online and followed the information before my first appointment; here, now, climbing the steps, I'm having second thoughts.

*Get it together, Sylvie. You've read all about waxing and even looked at photos online. Get your butt up these stairs; you're a grown-ass woman.*

My legs are weak on the final set of stairs, and my hand trembles when I reach toward the door handle. I pause before grabbing as I read the sign hanging from the knob that says, "Please take a seat. I'll be with you shortly."

Sitting in the little waiting area in one of the two chairs, my nerves skyrocket, while my knee bounces. The door opens and I'm summoned to enter, remove everything from my waist down, sit on the end of the table, place the towel across my lap, and wait. She'll be back shortly, she tells me.

"You're a new client. Have you waxed before?" the spa woman asks when she comes back.

"No."

"Do you know what style you want?" she asks next.

I flash back to the research I conducted on the web and the options. "I'd like to leave a landing strip," I nervously answer.

"Okay. I'll warn you: the wax is hot but safe. Remember to breathe; holding your breath won't help." Her back turns to me as she rolls a cart toward the table I lay on. "Ready?"

I nod, and she begins. I anticipated it would hurt more than it does, and I breathe a sigh of relief. We carry on a polite conversation as she applies the hot wax, smooths a strip upon it, and rips it off over and over again.

"Alright. Now, I need you to bend your knees, wrap your arms under them, then roll back on the table."

This I wasn't prepared for; everything is exposed. Every little bit of me is on display, and she wastes no time waxing every inch.

*Will I do this again?* I'm conflicted. It's weird, baring myself in this way to the esthetician. It's kind of like a pelvic exam without the cold, clinical feel. I'm really not sure how I feel about it. Walking back to my car, I look at my phone screen.

*No way!* The appointment lasted only 10 minutes. *That was easy.*

---

Early the next morning, Dawn and I sip our coffee poolside.

"Get this," I begin. "Last night, I was sitting at the bar of the Brickhouse, listening to live music, when *he* happened to sit on the stool beside me. We were both surprised that we share a love of the same music. We talked a lot, and that's when he asked me out on a date." With wide eyes, I look to Dawn, anxious to hear her thoughts.

She leans closer to me, her eyes twinkling. "Where'd he want to take you?"

I chuckle. "It's funny really. He asked to take me to the State Fair on Thursday."

"And you think *that* is funny?" Dawn quirks a perfectly-maintained eyebrow at me.

"Well, I actually have two VIP passes and tickets to the Communicable concert that same night at the fair."

"No way!" She stands upright, mouth agape.

"I planned to bribe Lidia to attend with me," I share. "It's not her type of music, but I didn't want to go alone."

"So, he's taking you to the State Fair, and you're taking him to the concert," Dawn summarizes, and I nod. "Wow. I can't wait to hear all of the hot details of the date?"

## Chapter Forty-Nine
# STEPHEN

"Hi, young hottie!" Dawn yells toward me as she scurries from her front porch toward Sylvie's driveway. I'm sure I turn three shades of red.

It's Thursday afternoon, and I suppose she's been glued to her front window and security camera app most of the afternoon. Sylvie warned me about Dawn's voyeuristic capabilities.

While I love that her cameras help keep Sylvie safe, I fear her keeping tabs on us might get annoying. I chat on the lawn with Dawn for a couple of minutes before Sylvie emerges from the front door, rescuing me.

*Damn! Sylvie's a sexy little minx.*

"You look..." I chuckle, not sure how to convey she's hot without sounding like a teenager.

With soft spikes on the crown of her head and wispy, short curls on the sides and back, this is my favorite way she styles her hair. While she's a natural beauty, I enjoy the allure of her smokey eyes and pale pink cheeks that match her lip gloss.

My eyes catch on her sun-kissed shoulders, bared by her black halter top. The silver, metal grommets lining the neck bring back memories of her and the motorcycle. Her denim, cutoff shorts perfectly hug her hips and ass, while the hemline is at a respectable length. In my mind, I imagine they're an inch or two shorter, allowing some of her cheeks to peek out. I brush away that thought. I wouldn't want her on display like that in public; that's for my eyes only.

*Is it too early in the relationship to claim her as mine?*

The heels of her lace-up sandals cause her tan calves to pop deliciously. I long to feel her long legs wrapped around my waist.

*This may be a long night.*

"Ready?" Sylvie asks, patting my shoulder, drawing my attention back to the present.

"You two kids have fun," Dawn calls, walking back toward her yard.

I place my hand in the small of Sylvie's back, ushering her to the passenger door of my truck. Pulling the door open, I lean my mouth to her ear.

"You look amazing," I murmur, fighting the urge to put my hands on her hips to lift her up into the cab.

"Thanks." She smiles, looking at me over her shoulder. Then, with her hand on the "oh, shit" handle, she pulls herself into the truck.

On the road, I blabber to avoid awkward silences. "I've arranged to park in an officer's yard that lives a block from the fairgrounds," I share. "It's a prime location, and they make a lot of money renting out parking spots during the state fair."

"Parking is crazy; I hope your buddy still has one available," Sylvie states.

"I called mid-week, and he agreed to save us one for tonight," I explain.

"Lucky us," Sylvie smiles.

*I love the way her eyes light up when she smiles. Like. Like. I like the way they light up.*

## Chapter Fifty
# SYLVIE

"So, be honest," I begin while he drives. "Are you a fan of Communicable?"

"Honestly," he says, glancing in my direction then back to the road before him, "I could only name three of their songs. When I downloaded their album to prepare for tonight, I realized I know several more than I thought."

*I'm lucky he likes metal and rock. Lidia would have been bored tonight.*

"I still can't believe you purchased two VIP packages to see Communicable," he says, eyes remaining on the road.

I'm grateful he doesn't ask or want to know how much I paid. I wanted to make up for all of the concerts I've missed in my past, so I paid $1,700 per person, so $3,400 plus the processing fees.

*I'm worth it.*

I remind him, "I planned to invite Lidia to attend with me, but it's not her type of music."

My excitement grows with every step we take on our way into the fair and the outdoor grandstand. Our paper tickets are exchanged for lanyards. Placing it around my neck sends my adrenaline into overdrive. As a free drink bracelet wraps around my wrist, I take a peek at my hand. Sure enough, it trembles.

With his band secured, Stephen places his hand in mine, and murmurs, "I feel like I can't breathe."

My eyes meet his. His excitement helps to calm my nerves a bit. I don't want to embarrass myself by turning into a fangirl.

We're led with one other couple to meet the band in a green room of sorts. Each of us takes a turn posing for a photo, standing between lead singer, Warner Bradshaw, and lead guitarist, Carson Cavanaugh. When they find out we're a couple, Carson pulls us together for a photo with both of us in it, then—even though it's only two hours before the show—the drinks flow.

Scanning the room, I note every member of the band is here. Two women stand near the door, attention glued to their tablets with an occasional hand to the headset over their ear. *They must be with the band.* Four young men lean on the bar, talking animatedly. I recognize two as the drummer, Eli, and the bassist, Jake. Three other men in suits mill about, sticking out like sore thumbs. *No way they're with the band dressed like that.*

"Enjoy yourself," Stephens murmurs near my ear, pointing toward the bar. "I'll have a couple then stop before the concert so I can drive home."

I love that he's conscious of that and wants us to have a good time.

I text Lidia, begging her to take a screenshot of any Snaps I send her, so I'll get a copy to keep. Then, I Snapchat a few photos: sitting on the sofa beside Warner Bradshaw, chatting with Jake Johnson, and taking a shot with Carson Cavanaugh and his wife, Montana.

When the band claims this is their first time performing in Iowa, I correct them. "Not true. You performed at the Brickhouse while recording two summers ago."

"Burn" one of the other fans taunts.

"Montana claims this is the best state fair in the country," Eli mentions, motioning to Carson's wife.

"The fair has a huge following," Stephen answers. "Morning shows from New York travel here to air from the fair for a week. Heck, the entire state practically shuts down during the fair. You should find time to check it out before you move on."

"Not to pressure you into it," I taunt. "Stephen Tyler walked the midway and rode a couple rides after he performed here a couple of years ago." I bite my lower lip. I can't believe I am in a private room with the members of Communicable and am taunting them as if we're longtime friends.

"Let's do it," Eli and Jake encourage in unison.

I shrug, smiling while inside, I have butterflies at the thought of witnessing the band at the fair like Iowa residents.

"Best date ever," Stephen whispers, leaning into my neck.

## Chapter Fifty-One
# SYLVIE

My skin prickles, and my body hums with his nearness. It's familiar and feels like we've been together forever. Turning in his direction, I smile. His eyes drop to my mouth then back to my eyes. In them, I see his want. A minuscule movement is all the confirmation he needs.

The moment his lips crush to mine, a jolt of lightning zings through me. He keeps it short and leaves me wanting more. I'm still floating in the clouds when it's announced we need to make our way to our seats. I follow Stephen's lead as I try to gather my wits.

He grabs each of us a beer, and we find our seats. There are only four of us in the entire grandstand; it's both eerie and exciting. Our tickets are in the third row, where we find our free tour t-shirts waiting for us.

Iowa's oppressive August heat remains heavy in the air this evening. Stephen looks miserably sexy. His face glistens with sweat, which he constantly swipes away. It's not easy for all guys to dress appropriately for this weather. I can't imagine him in shorts or sandals. A white, short-sleeved tee stretches across his broad shoulders, his arm muscles threatening to burst out of the straining sleeves. His fitted jeans add to his discomfort in this heat, while the fabric hugs his ass and thighs.

I laughed so hard I snorted when I read his T-shirt in my driveway. "I'm with the band." Stephen is not only gorgeous with a capital 'G'; he's funny, protective, and astute.

*Yummy. I'm one lucky woman—at least for tonight.*

---

As the crowd fills the grandstand, I notice fans in the rows around us are all younger than me.

"Let's send a pic to Lidia," I say, offering my phone to him.

Thank goodness he's a pro. He knows to move the phone so that the stage shows behind us. With his long arms, he easily takes the selfie.

A woman in the row behind ours offers to take a photo of the two of us. I gladly pass her my phone.

## Chapter Fifty-Two
# STEPHEN

In this photo, I place my arm around Sylvie's waist and pull her tight to my side. The smell of her vanilla-scented skin mixed with the musk of her sweat tickles my nostrils. Her long, lean body molds to mine like two pieces of a puzzle.

I've only posed for photos with my sister and my nieces. With Sylvie, I don't mind. In fact, I want everyone to know she's with me. *She's mine.*

*Whoa! Where did that come from?* I don't date. I choose one-night stands. I don't pose for photos that might send the wrong message to the woman. Sylvie's different; I gravitate towards her.

*How is it possible that she instantly changed everything?* She makes me want to try. Try to date. Try to have a relationship. Try to be a couple in public. She's magnetic; she's my kryptonite.

I release her, and we turn to face the stage. Roadies scurry here and there, then disappear. Sylvie bounces on her tiptoes, her hands clasped in front of her chin, and her eyes wide. She holds nothing back; she's a breath of fresh air.

---

Song after song, Communicable delivers. The electric crowd, paired with Sylvie's belting out every lyric, plants a permanent smile upon my face.

As the opening notes of a ballad fill the air, I shift my body behind hers. I place my hands on her hips as she sways gently to the music. She allows her head to lay upon my chest, and her body presses back into mine while we continue to move as one.

*That's it. The end. I'm a goner.* The sensation of her body pressed back into mine from shoulder to thigh spirals my desire. I no longer hear the band. I no longer hear the crowd. It's only Sylvie and me, swaying in unison.

---

"Should we stroll the midway before we go?" I offer, my lips grazing her ear as we shuffle slowly with the crowd toward the exit.

Sylvie tips her head back, allowing me to gaze into her hazel-colored eyes. For once, my number one concern is not assessing the crowd for danger. I focus my attention on her —on touching her, on holding her, and on everything I long to do with her.

"Let's ride the Ferris wheel," she urges.

I find it hard to deny her anything.

As our car slowly rises above the hordes of people below

us, I wonder how many times she's ridden this ride and if she's ever been kissed high above the fairgrounds below.

"Did 17-year-old Sylvie ride the Ferris wheel every year, enjoying kisses in the night?" It's out there before I can think better of it.

She scoots her body closer in suggestion. "No, but I'm up to share my first Ferris wheel kiss with you."

## Chapter Fifty-Three
# SYLVIE

Too soon, the warm sunlight bathes my face upon my pillow. I mew, stretching my deliciously sore body, the sheet falling to my side. I freeze, memories of last night scrolling through my mind. My eyes fly open to find a condom box upon my nightstand.

*No!*

"Good morning," Stephen's gravelly voice greets.

"Umm," I turn my head then clutch the sheet over my chest as my body turns to face him.

He lifts his hand, his fingers brushing a stray hair strand from my forehead.

"I, uh..." I struggle to put together a coherent thought. His bare chest and scruffy jawline obliterate all thought.

Several moments pass until I find my words. "So, that happened," I blurt.

He bites his lips together, his eyes dancing.

"This isn't me," I state. "I haven't dated in over 25 years, and a lot has changed. You may be used to this type of dating, but I'm not. I wasn't, and I'm still not a sleep-with-a-guy-on-the-first-date, one-night stand type of woman."

"I don't consider this our first date," he smirks, his soft, sleepy eyes on mine.

*Seriously? He wants to argue?*

"The Brickhouse was more like a first date, and you already know I kind of feel Zoo Brew and bike night were mini-dates." His dark brown eyes lock on mine. "I learned more about you at each event," he adds as explanation.

"Ha," I choke. "I already knew you were a cop, so I didn't learn anything new from you at Zoo Brew and bike night," I counter.

"I feel..." He rolls his entire body to face me. "It feels as if I've known you for months or even years. I can't explain it. There's so much I don't know about you, yet you seem familiar."

I know what he means. I feel the same, as if he's my...*soulmate*. I attempt to swallow the lump in my throat. *Too soon. It's too soon for all of this.*

He rests his palm upon my cheek. "I don't plan to fight this, whatever is between us. Something started the night I delivered the noise complaint to you, and try as I might, it didn't fade; you've kept popping up in my life."

"I..." I sputter. "I've never..."

He releases my cheek, shaking his head. "This is new for me, too." He raises up on an elbow. "I don't fall asleep or spend the night." He looks towards the ceiling then back. "I'm drawn to you in a way I can't bring myself to leave." He shrugs. "I like to keep things casual—I have to with my job. I haven't let myself be in a relationship; my work is too dangerous."

I place my palm on his chest near his heart. "Officers deserve families; you deserve it all. Your career path doesn't change that. It's not fair—"

He cuts me off. "I live day to day because I can't promise to come home at the end of each shift. I can't control criminals and can't ask anyone—"

I interrupt, "Then, don't ask. Allow." My eyes implore him to really hear me. "Allow others to choose to be in your life. Other officers have families."

"Many Iowans have a false sense of security," he explains, his hand resting over mine. "Crime exists here just like everywhere else in this country. People are unpredictable, and with the rising incidents in the mental health crisis, it's even more unstable. I do my best to keep safe—the thought of asking a woman, let alone children, to live with that uncertainty... I won't let myself be that selfish."

I squint at him in front of me. "You're hiding behind that excuse." I state. "You're trying to protect yourself—not others."

He shakes his head. "I should leave. Hell, I should have left hours ago." He chuckles. "I couldn't bring myself to let go of you. This..." he moves his index finger back and forth between us. "This is different; it's new to me."

"Then, *let* it be different. Don't push me away. Don't try to protect me from your job."

*What the hell am I saying? Am I ready? Do I want to be in a relationship?* It's not like me to jump in the deep end.

"Just let it be," he smiles. "It's that easy, huh?"

"Yep. I'll make a deal with you," I smile back. "I won't fight it if you won't."

I watch his Adam's apple move as he swallows hard. He nods, pulls me close, and his mouth collides with mine.

---

## Stephen

"Look away, please," Sylvie murmurs.

"Uh-huh," I argue.

"C'mon," she pleads.

"Don't be shy," I prompt.

She shakes her head, and her eyes turn downward. I place my forefinger under her chin, lifting her eyes back to mine. Her tongue darts out to wet her lower lip, before her teeth tug on it. It's easy to guess she doesn't want me to see her naked, now that it's day. The confident woman, holding nothing back while seeking her orgasm of last night is no more. Next to me she now clutches the sheet tightly to her chest.

"Syl..."

"I'm...I..." she stammers. "I'm not in my 20s and my body..."

"Hey," I murmur, reaching for her. "I like *every* part of you." I tilt her face up to mine. "No one's perfect. I'm not perfect. You're beautiful inside and out. I want to learn every curve, every scar."

She shakes her head.

"I'll close my eyes," I offer, placing my hand over my eyes.

When she giggles, I peek between my fingers. She's darting into the attached bathroom, but I catch a glace of her long lean body and round ass. Perfect. She's perfect. She has nothing to hide, but I won't push her.

## Chapter Fifty-Four
# SYLVIE

Breakfast dishes barely in the dishwasher, Stephen orders, "Give me a tour of your studio." Then, he pulls me with him.

"There's really not much to see," I state, passing him to take the lead.

I pull the French doors open. I'm suddenly nervous about sharing my happy place with him. I fear it might seem silly to a non-painter.

"Pardon the mess," I murmur. "It's organized and makes sense to me."

"Show me," he says, lifting his chin toward the white canvas on the easel. "I want to see you paint."

I take a palette in hand, squeeze a dab of royal blue and black onto it, and grab a nearby brush. I move in front of the blank canvas. Stephen moves behind me; I feel his warm breath upon my neck.

I mix some blue with a tiny bit of black paint, and I add a bit more blue with my brush. I place my brush on the canvas and look over my shoulder at Stephen. Uncomfortable with his smoldering dark eyes, I must force myself to look away. I slowly begin with a wide stroke and gently taper it as it curves. Stephen's right hand covers mine. Together, we continue pressing the dark blue upon the canvas. His warm lips press to the nape of my neck. His tongue darts out to wet my skin then he blows, prickling my skin.

"That's not how to paint," my husky voice informs him.

He takes my brush and palette. I turn to find a sexy smirk upon his face as he places the brush upon the tip of my nose.

"Hey," I admonish.

He proceeds to dab paint on each of my cheeks.

"This means war," I declare.

"Wait," he begs, backing away. "Let me remove my white shirt and shoes. And you should remove your jeans."

Both stripped to our underwear, I grab paint and a brush to defend myself.

## Chapter Fifty-Five
# STEPHEN

I'm frozen in place, paintbrush in my hand. Sylvie stands in a dainty pastel pink bra and panty set with blue paint on the tip of her nose and each cheek. The image of her like this will be burned in my memory forever.

I could get used to this, spending our evenings out on the town, falling into bed in each other's arms, eating breakfast together, and playing for the rest of the day. I could, but I won't. I'll dabble a little, dip my toe in the proverbial pool, but I won't go all in. I won't allow myself to hurt her.

"1...2..." she taunts.

"3!" I lunge forward, paintbrush extended, and miss.

Sylvie ducks, slathering my thighs with quick, sideways strokes.

"Gotcha!" she announces, standing behind me.

"Damn, you're fast." I laugh, turning.

She expertly paints my back, my neck, and my ribs.

Clearly, I'm out of my league here. I'm distracted. *That's what it is.* I'm allowing my body's reaction to her to slow me down.

"Come here," I order, wrapping my hand around the wrist of the hand holding her brush.

Flush against me, she attempts to wiggle free. She struggles for only a moment, freezing when my fingers unclasp her bra. Her mouth opens, and a gasp escapes. My eyes move from her perfect pale pink lips to her hazel eyes.

Now, I have the upper hand. With one arm holding her tight to my chest, the other guides the paint brush slowly up her spine.

"Mmm..." she moans, her body relaxing into mine.

I push the straps of her bra off her shoulders. She arches her back, allowing her heavy breasts to free from their silky cups. Stealing her brush, I hold two paintbrushes a hairsbreadth from her nipples. The pale pink nubs harden, straining to reach the bristles with her heaving breaths. Simultaneously, I paint each tip, swirl over the areola, then pinch each nipple between my thumb and brush handle. I marvel at her complete trust and unabashed desire.

"Mmm..." she moans again, eyes closed, basking in the sensations.

I paint a trail under each breast, down her ribs, and to her navel, causing her heavy-lidded eyes to open. I tickle her lower abdomen, stroking side to side. Goosebumps rise, and her breath hitches.

The two brushes fall to the floor, allowing my fingertips to dive beneath the waistband of her panties. Eyes locked on hers, I ease closer and closer to the apex of her thighs.

She holds her breath in anticipation. I search her eyes for permission, then slip my index finger between her hot, wet folds. Slowly, her eyes close, and her tongue peeks out to swipe her lower lip. Gently I slide my finger down her seam, my thumb rubbing her clit. On contact with her bundle of nerves, her knees bend. Out of fear of her falling, I place my free hand on the small of her back.

Moments pass before Sylvie, while still enjoying my ministrations, moves her hands from my shoulders down my chest to pause on my abdomen. Ready to explode, I change our position. On my knees, I slide her panties down her thighs and calves before she steps free of them. I tug on her forearms, encouraging her to join me on the canvas covering her floor.

She tugs my boxer briefs down my legs before climbing over me. Her knees planted on either side of me, one hand on my chest, she slowly lowers herself upon my rock-hard cock. She pauses with an inch to go, allowing her body time to acclimate to my girth.

"Wait. Condom," I warn, my hands pressed to her thighs.

Sylvie shakes her head. "I can't get pregnant, remember?"

My over-stimulated brain scurries to recall such a conversation. *Only one child, didn't want more, got a tubal...* I nod, my body on high alert. I've never not worn a condom. No condom means no barrier, and no barrier means more pleasure.

"It's deeper," she groans, sliding further until I'm fully implanted within her hot center.

As my hands at her hips encourage her to move, I drum up all of my willpower to keep from losing my control too soon. Knowing I won't last long, I place the pad of my thumb on her swollen clit, swirling it in unison with her movements.

"Yes!" she moans loudly, grinding harder against me.

"Oh, my...Yes!" She yells through her groan. Her head is thrown back, her back arched.

Wave after wave, her orgasm constricts my shaft. Hands still upon her hips, I drive into her, once, twice, then a third time. I shudder, a full body tremor as I lose every last drop into her.

Forcing my hands to relax their grip on her hips, I will my eyes to open. I find Sylvie looking down on me, a soft smile on her face as she bites her lower lip. Her hands fall off my chest, her elbows bend, and her torso meets mine.

"Best. First. Date. Ever," I state, my mouth near her ear.

Her body bounces with her laughter.

---

Moments after Stephen leaves, I stand staring at the paint smears upon the drop cloth on my studio floor. Two fingers press against my lips, my belly warms, and my cheeks head as I replay the scene of our bodies, our pleasure, creating this masterpiece. I need to keep it; I long to save this memory.

*I could make a blanket or pillow covers; the tan cloth with its blue and black patterns is large. Or I could stretch the cloth over a large canvas to display on the bare wall above my bed.*

I bite my lap, a smile growing. I like the idea of it as the last thing I see at night and it greeting me every morning. Its story will be my little secret.

## Chapter Fifty-Six
# SYLVIE

I'm thankful to be assisting Stephen with his partner's kids in my pool this afternoon. If alone I fear I might have spent the entire day convincing myself that I shouldn't be dating anyone, let alone someone 14 years younger than me.

When he informed me he offered to watch Fredrick's three kids today, I insisted he bring them over to enjoy my pool. So, here we are, Stephen and the three kids in my pool as I sit in the sun, attempting to dry off a bit before I let the dogs out of their kennels to join us in the backyard.

While six-year-old Winston and eight-year-old Michelle scamper about, the youngest boy, Daniel remains within arm's reach of Stephen at all times. He has pool floaties on each of his arms, but Stephen assures me he knows how to swim without them.

Before he left to pick up the kids today, he shared that at age 5, Daniel is nonverbal and struggles to socialize with strangers. This is one of the reasons Stephen volunteers to watch the kids, as finding a sitter is hard for them.

While I hoped having his siblings and Stephen here might make him more comfortable, Daniel still hasn't looked my way or interacted with me.

When I slip into the house, I allow my two dogs to follow me to the grass on one side of the backyard. "Go potty," I order, attempting to keep my body between Bo and the kids swimming in the pool, distracting him.

"Bo, go potty," I direct over and over until he complies.

"Good boy," I cheer, then slip both dogs a small treat.

We walk back toward the patio around the pool. Bo immediately whines at the pool's edge, standing near the children playing in the water.

"Let them in; it's no problem," Stephen says.

Daniel perks up, eyes glued on my puppy.

I lift Bo onto a mat to float, pushing him gently away from the edge.

Daniel ventures farther away from Stephen, eyes glued on Bo. Hovering nearby, he smiles, giving all of his attention to the puppy on the floating mat.

Not wanting to interrupt the fun, I wait as long as possible before I suggest everyone dry off so we can apply fresh sunscreen. Michelle and Winston take one more time off the diving board then swim to the ladder at the side of the pool.

Stephen guides Bo towards the pool steps and Daniel follows. Wrapping him in a towel, he prompts Daniel into a chair and places Bo beside him.

I apply lotion to the two older children then set a timer on my phone for when they may enter the water. Daniel refuses to drop his towel. Both Stephen and I try, but we aren't successful in applying more sunscreen. Even when Stephen enters the water, lifting Daniel's siblings over his head and tossing them into the deep end, Daniel remains wrapped tight in his towel in the shade of the patio umbrella.

Every part of me longs to talk to him, sit nearby, and entertain Daniel. But I don't. Instead, I give my attention to Hagrid and Bo.

## Chapter Fifty-Seven
# STEPHEN

"Sit," Sylvie directs. Hagrid sits, and she rewards him with a tiny training treat.

Daniel moves to the end of his lounge chair to better see Sylvie and the dogs.

Next, Sylvie looks to Bo. "Sit," she commands firmly. When Bo doesn't obey, she repeats, "Sit." She places her hand on his bottom, pushes it to the patio, then gives Bo a treat.

My breath catches when Daniel approaches them.

"You want to give him one?" Sylvie extends the small treat toward him. Daniel remains close but doesn't react. She gently opens his tiny hand, slips him a treat, then assists his fingers in closing.

My cell phone alarm signals it's time to go. Not wanting to interrupt Daniel's interaction with Sylvie and the dogs, I quickly silence my phone alarm and instruct Michelle and Winston to dry off.

"High five," Sylvie instructs Hagrid. He obeys and gets a treat.

"Bo," Sylvie directs her attention to the little hound, "high five." She helps the puppy give her a high five with one of his front paws then offers him a treat.

Next, she looks at her older dog. "Hagrid, sit." He obeys and receives a treat as reward.

"Bo, sit," Sylvie directs. With no reaction, she repeats, "Bo, sit."

"Bo! Sit!" Daniel orders.

In shock, Sylvie watches her puppy sit and receive a treat from the little boy. She turns to me, her mouth agape. A large lump in my throat and tears welling in my eyes, I stare back, awestruck. Michelle stands beside me, hand to her mouth and eyes wide.

I'm not sure how to react and decide to follow Sylvie and Michelle's lead. We stand, marveling at Bo and his miraculous effect on little Daniel. I snag my phone to record.

"Hagrid," Sylvie continues. "Lay down." Again, she rewards him for his compliance then passes the small treat bag to Daniel.

"Bo," Daniel orders, "way down." Daniel's little boy voice is firm.

The puppy tilts his little head, large ears flopping heavily.

"Bo, way down." Daniel points to the concrete.

Still nothing.

"Bo, sit." When the puppy sits, Daniel passes him a treat.

I sneak a peak in Winston's direction. He stands, wide-eyed, tucked under his big sister's arm.

Fighting tears, Sylvie smiles proudly in my direction.

Out of treats, Sylvie plops down on the patio, rubbing

Hagrid's belly. Nearby, Daniel mimics her actions. Bo crawls up on the little boy's lap, happy to accept his loves.

A wide smile upon my face, I mouth, "Oh. My. God."

Sylvie's smile assures me she understands the weight of this moment. This is a big deal.

## Chapter Fifty-Eight
# SYLVIE

My vibrating cell phone draws my attention from my painting.

**Stephen: Thought I'd pick up dinner & head your way**
**Me: What if I've already eaten?**
**Stephen: I'll bring dessert**
**Me: Bring dinner + dessert = it's a deal**
**Stephen: See ya soon**

Smiling widely, I put away my paint brush. I pause, admiring the bright sunshine and field of flowers I created while Stephen drove the children home. Daniel's words and interactions with Bo prompted my sunny, upbeat painting. I cover my canvas, preparing for his return.

Moments later, I'm exiting the bathroom when my doorbell rings.

"Wow. That was quick," I greet, opening the front door.

It's not Stephen. Crap! "I'm sorry. I thought you were someone else," I explain.

"Expecting Stephen?" the stranger asks, tucking her curly hair behind her ear.

I'm statue-still, holding the door open.

"I'm Elizabeth, Officer Calderon's wife," she explains. "My children enjoyed swimming with Stephen and you today."

"Where are my manners? C'mon in." I wave my free arm toward the living room.

"I don't want to intrude," she states, standing near the sofa. "I'll only need a minute."

"No problem," I reply, taking a seat in a nearby chair. "The kids had so much fun. I told Stephen we should invite your whole family over to grill and swim."

She nods. "I want to thank you. Stephen sent me the video..." Her voice cracks as her eyes fill with tears. "We'd hoped and prayed his silence was temporary. As year after year passed, the odds were not in our favor."

I nod, smiling, unable to speak due to the heavy lump in my throat.

"You're magic," Elizabeth claims, "an angel sent to us."

"He did all the work," I argue. "I was blessed to witness Daniel in action." I shake my head. "He decided when to use his words."

Her tears flow freely down her cheeks. "I believe in a higher power that guides our lives. I think your neighbor calling the police station was a catalyst to introduce Stephen to you and bring Daniel to your home."

*A higher power? Hmm...* I've always believed in fate and our destined paths. Whether it's a higher power, fate, or destiny, I'm honored Daniel entered my life on the day he spoke his first words.

"I wish you were here in my place," I confess, unsure what else to say.

"I've always told Stephen there was a perfect woman out there for him," she informs. "You're the perfect woman that Daniel felt safe enough with to open up and speak."

"Whoa..." I raise my hands, palms toward her. "I'm far from perfect, and we've only been on one date..."

Elizabeth quirks her head. "You chatted at the bar, you went to the concert, you babysat together, and he spent the night." She waggles her eyebrows suggestively. "He never, and I mean never, spends the night. And you are the first woman that he's talked about non-stop."

*He talks about me non-stop?* Apparently, he's told Fredrik and her everything.

"I probably should not have spilled the beans about that to you," she hedges.

I bite my lips and nearly hit the roof when my doorbell rings.

"That will be Stephen," she states, standing.

Stephen lets himself in. I don't have time to process that because I'm wrapped in a tight bear-hug. Wide-eyed, I look to Stephen.

"You'll never know how happy it makes me that you've entered our lives." She rocks me side to side, still clutching tightly. "Thank you for today."

I pull in a deep breath, free from her embrace. "I meant it when I said we should grill and chat while the kids swim. All of you are welcome any time."

Hagrid and Bo scratch at the patio door, curious about the two doorbell chimes, so I let them in.

"This must be Bo," Elizabeth states, lowering herself to the floor. "You are adorable. You're even cuter in person."

Bo climbs into her lap, enjoying her rubs. "He's so cute and those ears."

"He'll never grow into them," Stephen states. "Or his paws."

"Stop that," I admonish. "Basset hounds have long ears and big feet."

"Alright," Elizabeth stands. "As much as I want to stay and love this little cutie," she passes Bo to me, "I should get back home. You two have fun." She winks at me and pats Stephen's shoulder.

"Don't let the door hit you on the way out," Stephen says.

## Chapter Fifty-Nine
# SYLVIE

"Be nice," I chide, waving to Elizabeth as she slips through the door. "She came over to introduce herself and thank me. I told her it wasn't anything I did. Daniel did it himself."

In two long strides, Stephen wraps his arms around me, pulling me flush against his chest. "Don't argue with me; just listen." His voice drops low. "You have this way of making everyone around you feel comfortable. I feel it, the kids feel it..." He places a kiss on the top of my head. "Daniel relaxed today. That's not usually the case for him. He refuses to engage in new situations and people."

"But you were here," I argue.

"Ah, ah, ah," he teases. "It's listening time for you. Usually, he glues himself to his parents, his sister, or me. He didn't do that. He moved around the pool on his own, swimming closer and closer to the dogs. You have this calm—I don't know, maybe it's a calm aura—around you. Instead of shutting you out, he watched you. He chose to approach you and the dogs. He mimicked your behaviors. He doesn't do that with someone he just met. He doesn't approach animals, either. So, whether you choose to believe it or not, you were partially responsible for him speaking."

He squeezes me tighter, and I tighten my hold on him. Several quiet moments pass.

"She thinks I've found my perfect match," he whispers. "Now that she's met you, I'll never hear the end of it. She already warns me not to do anything to screw this up."

I lift my head from his shoulder, looking up to him through my lashes. "After one date?" I shake my head slightly. "Is she this way with all of your dates?"

He smiles a sexy little grin. "I told you, I don't date. I definitely don't share details of my hookups either." His eyes ping-pong from mine to my mouth and back. "She claims I had 'a glow' about me this morning." He makes air quotes. "She knew I had a date last night and recognized I wore the same clothes from the pics we sent her husband with the band. She's very perceptive."

I bite my lips.

"She went on and on about all the ways I'm different when I talk about you..."

I interrupt, "You didn't tell her about last night, did you?"

"No," he states, leaving no doubt. "She put two and two together. I did share details about our time swimming with the kids."

"She argued with me when I stated we'd only been on one date," I share.

"How many times must I tell you? We've had other dates!"

I pull away from him, shaking my head once again.

"What's for dinner?" I ask, changing the subject.

Stephen's smirk assures me he knows what I'm doing. "I made an executive decision. We're skipping dinner and going straight to dessert."

## Chapter Sixty
# STEPHEN

"I enjoyed today," I inform Sylvie as we eat our second bowl of ice cream.

"The kids are so adorable," she mumbles, ice cream still in her mouth.

"I bet they'll hound Fredrik and Elizabeth nonstop to come swim again," I chuckle.

Mouth empty, Sylvie swallows a sip of water. "What a rush. I mean... It was my first time with Daniel, but knowing he spoke for the first time... What a rush."

I nod; there are no words to describe the monumental moment we witnessed.

"You're so good with the kids," she continues. "And it's clear they absolutely love spending time with you." She smiles fondly.

I fear I know where she's headed with this line of conversation. "Like I've shared before, I like being around other people's children. I love what I do. And to continue loving it, I can't have children." My eyes lock on hers.

"But..."

"So..." I interrupt her, drawing it out. "that's the reason for my vasectomy. I may be greedy, but I won't let my love of career cause stress or pain to children."

"You told me I wasn't greedy in making my decision. Thus, you aren't greedy for making the same decision." Sylvie smirks, tossing my words back at me. "I was just making an observation, not trying to force the issue. Besides..." She bites her lips, her eyes purposefully looking away from mine. "If you wanted children of your own, we'd be through."

Snagging her wrist, I pull her onto my lap. "I'm enjoying this relationship thing. I'm in no hurry to move on."

Clearly, my words didn't convey the meaning I'd hoped. I cup her chin, turning her to face me. "I need you to understand what I'm trying to tell you." I wet my lips, loving her eyes focused on my mouth. "I'm having fun."

*Crap! That sounds bad.*

"Urgh..." I growl. "I'm into you. I want to spend as much time as I can with you. I'm here until you tire of me."

My eyes beg her to understand I'm on the verge of sharing three little words out loud. I've never spoken them to anyone aside from my family, and I worry if I say them, I'll scare her away. I'm not sure if there are unspoken rules or a timeline for relationships. *Man, relationships are much harder than I ever dreamed.*

"I..." I sputter nervously. "I... I like you." My heart rate skyrockets. "I probably like you more than I should for the amount of time we've spent together."

Her eyes glisten as a wide smile graces her face. Her reaction, while unexpected, is very welcome. I urge her to stand with me, place my hands on each of her cheeks, and gaze into her eyes.

"It's not too soon," she whispers, eyes locked on mine. "I'm fighting it, too."

We don't speak the three words we're dancing around.

On their own, my lips find hers. My mouth consumes her; my tongue tastes all she has to give. My lungs protest eventually, and I'm forced to end our kiss. Forehead to forehead, we struggle to pull in air.

"I'm falling in love with you," I admit in a whisper. "I'm done trying to deny it, and I pray I didn't just scare you away."

Sylvie leans her body tighter to mine. She places a kiss on my chin, my jaw, then the corner of my mouth. She lifts a leg, her thigh grazing deliciously against my swelling cock. She doesn't parrot my sentiment, choosing to show me instead.

## Chapter Sixty-One
# SYLVIE

I stand before my vanity, taking in my reflection. I marvel at the woman I've become. I love sex. I think about sex with Stephen twenty-four-seven. It's not the fact it's been missing from my life since my early twenties, it's Stephen. I can't get enough of him. I fantasize about his lips tasting every inch of my skin, the rough pads of his fingers grazing over my sensitive parts, and his cock. What a cock! I should be alarmed at how much time I spend thinking of his cock and the magical things it does to me.

*Crap! I'm doing it again.* I roll my eyes at my hard nipples poking into my vintage Nirvana tee. I rub my thighs together, attempting to quell the damp heat of my core. Vibrator. This calls for my vibrator. I step from the bathroom toward my bed. I pause, my hand on the knob to my nightstand.

Harness it. Harness these feelings and place them on a canvas. Paint. I must paint.

My vibrating phone jolts me from my painting. I hurry to my table, placing my paint brush on a nearby paper plate. My body hums with excitement to read what Stephen texts.

**Lidia: got an A**

I sigh disappointed it's not from Stephen. It's stupid; his shift doesn't end for two more hours. She's my daughter for Pete's sake. Her texts should be the most important. *What kind of mother gets disappointed by a text from her only child?* Shaking my head, I process the text I received.

**Me: Awesome job!**
**Me: 1 more to go**
**Lidia: easy 1 left**
**Me: 1 more A?**
**Lidia: that's the goal**
**Me: good luck & keep me posted**
**Lidia: will do**

I should try to remain distant, instead of fall head over heels so fast. I shake my head, knowing I can't change my feelings.

There's something about Stephen that draws me to him. It's useless to fight it, and I don't want to fight it. I like how he makes me feel and I like how I am in his presence.

## *Chapter Sixty-Two*
# SYLVIE

I glance at my cell phone clock; it's almost eleven. My insides cheer as I prepare for his text. My thumbs hover over my screen. I'll shoot him a text. He tends to text me as soon as his shift ends, then again when he arrives home. I'll text him first tonight.

**Me: any noise complaints today?**
**Me: (laughing emoji)**

I return my phone on the table, grasp my paint brush, and stand at my easel. I purse my lips. The creative juices fled; I no longer feel the urge to paint. After cleaning my brushes and palette, I stand in the living room, staring at my phone. It's eleven-fifteen and no text from him yet. I'm rethinking my silly texts. Perhaps I messed up. I should've let him text me first. It's his thing and I...

My cell phone vibrates in my hand, causing my heartbeat to speed and my body to hum.

**Stephen: I wish**
**Stephen: worked out well for me last time**
**Me: looking to replace me already?**
**Stephen: never be a call like the 1 that brought me to u!**

I can't think of a witty reply.

**Stephen: (kissing emoji)**
**Stephen: headed your way**

*Wait. What?* I quickly scan myself head to toe. I'm a disheveled, paint-covered mess. I turn towards the hallway then back to the front door. My feet are cemented to the spot. I need a shower but there's not time. He'll be here...

*Crap!* I hear the thunk of his truck door closing in my driveway. Stunned I walk to my door. I unlock and open it as Stephen prepares to knock.

"I thought you didn't text while driving," I greet.

He laughs. He actually laughs at me.

"I used the hands-free talk to text today," he explains. "Did I catch you in the middle of something?" He points to my face and paint covered shirt.

"No, but you didn't give me time to clean up," I inform. "I'm a mess."

"Nope," he argues. "You're cute." His thumb wipes a paint smudge on my cheek.

*Cute? Do I want to be cute?*

Forefinger to my crinkled brow, Stephen asks, "What's going on up here?"

I attempt to shake off the topic, but he insists I share. "I'm not sure I want to be 'cute'." I make air quotes as I speak.

He chuckles. "Bull Durham, right?"

Tilting my head to the side, my eyes squint as I search for his meaning.

"You know the quote from Bull Durham," he prompts.

"Never watched it," I confess with a shrug.

"No way!" He stands mouth agape and his eyes wide.

I shrug again.

"Well, I'll make it my mission to remedy that as soon as possible," he states, pulling me into a hug. "Let's snack and then we will watch it."

I arch my back, smiling up at him.

"You didn't have any other plans, did you?" He grins down at me.

Text or videocall with him, I think to myself. I love that he wants to share a favorite movie with me. Secretly, I hope he will share all of his favorites with me, as well as take me to his favorite spots and restaurants. I long to experience everything with him.

## Chapter Sixty-Three
# STEPHEN

It's Thursday, I'm off, and today, I'm walking the zoo with Sylvie. I've been intrigued by her comments from the evening she bumped into us working Zoo Brew. I'm dying to experience the entire zoo with her.

Walking side by side, hand in hand, we turn left from the entrance.

"Maybe we'll catch a glimpse of some Animal Planet action." She giggles excitedly as we pass the first exhibit of flamingos.

I shake my head and can't help the big grin upon my face. Try as I might, I can't ever predict what she'll say or do next.

"What's your favorite animal?" I ask while we admire the river otters' agile swimming maneuvers.

"At this zoo or world-wide?" she inquires.

"World-wide," I answer, kissing the back of her hand in mine.

"I love hippos. They're awkward-looking but deadly

beasts in water," she answers without taking time to ponder. "Big cats fascinate me. I don't consider myself a cat person, but I love big cats. They are beautiful, graceful, powerful killing machines."

We walk away from the otters up a slight incline and stop at the bald eagle enclosure.

"Oh, and I'm intrigued by the new rhinos here." Sylvie squints as she takes in the enormous bird perched mere feet from us. "Talk about awkward. They're just weird to look at." She turns to face me, my forearms leaning on the metal bar around the eagle's cage, fencing her in. "Did you know they can't see? I mean, they aren't blind, but everything is very blurry for them."

I refrain from shaking my head at her. Instead, I place a kiss in the middle of her forehead. She wraps her arms around my waist. Her bright hazel eyes gaze at me through her lashes. Her teeth bite the corner of her lower lip. I try to refrain from laughing and fail miserably. She wants to tell me another fact; I can see her biting her lip to stop herself.

"I'm a nerd," she murmurs.

I nod. "I wouldn't have it any other way," I admit. "And I did know about the rhinos. I've brought my nieces and nephews here several times."

She turns back toward the majestic bird, leaning her head on my shoulder.

"The first time I saw this guy," she lifts her chin towards the bald eagle, "I was surprised by how large he was. I've seen them flying in our area during winter and perching in trees. They didn't look this big." I feel her shrug against my side. "I guess I thought I was closer to them than I really was. It's an optical illusion."

Hands on her hips, I spin her to face me. With a sudden awareness of several children around us, I refrain from melding my mouth with hers. Her eyes on my mouth, her tongue sweeps over her lower lip. My insides warm, knowing she desires me as I do her.

## Chapter Sixty-Four
# STEPHEN

"Daniel's gonna love her," Sylvie states in between little puppy licks and her giggles.

I struggle to keep my attention on the road. It's a constant struggle to focus on anything when I'm in her presence. She's all-consuming.

"Should we name her?' Sylvie holds the puppy at armslength near the dash.

I smile in her direction, then quickly return my eyes to the street before us.

"I know, I know," she continues. "Daniel's been talking more each day. She's just too cute. Yes, you are." She coos at the female Basset hound in her arms. "I'm glad Fredrik and Elizabeth chose to get him a puppy."

"I still can't believe you found them a free dog." I reply. "Runt or not, she's purebred and worth something."

"When I explained about Daniel's first words with Bocephus, she offered this little cutie to encourage Daniel to interact and speak more. She was excited to donate her as a therapy dog."

"You had a lot to do with it," I state, enamored by the affect she has on people. I put my truck in park. "Let's go surprise Daniel."

---

"What should we name her?" Daniel's sister Michelle asks him.

"Ten-a-the," He immediately answers.

All eyes turn to him, several brows raise, and confusion consumes all.

"What, honey?" Elizabeth asks.

"Ten-a-the," he states, pointing to the top of the refrigerator.

Beside me, Stephen bounces with quiet laughter. I elbow him in the ribs.

"What's funny?" I whisper.

Unable to speak, Stephen shakes his head.

Elizabeth walks toward the fridge, looking for the object Daniel points at. "Show me," she prompts.

"Daddy jui-th," Daniel points above the freezer.

"Fredrik!" she calls, stern voice raised.

Stephen's laughter continues, so I elbow him harder this time.

I watch Elizabeth chew Fredrik out, hands moving wildly between them.

"What's going on?" I whisper.

"They learned this week that Daniel can read. Like, really read. Fredrik and I sipped from his bottle of Jack Daniels night before last. Seems Daniel saw the bottle and now wants to name his puppy Tennessee," he chuckles. "We were supposed to be watching the kids not drinking."

I can't help but giggle. I love this family and Stephen's involvement with them. He's more than a friend, he's family.

## Chapter Sixty-Five
# STEPHEN

It's late Friday morning, and we've left the comfort of Sylvie's bed in search of sustenance. Sylvie hops up to sit on the counter between the stove and the refrigerator. I let the dogs in through the patio door then lean my hips against the kitchen island, facing her.

"Now what?" she asks, head cocked to one side, fingers strumming the granite countertop beside her exposed thighs peeking out from under my t-shirt.

I smirk. She's the cutest thing I've ever seen.

"My breakfast is typically a protein bar," she states. "I have a couple of eggs; we could whip up an omelet, or..."

I take this opportunity to demonstrate exactly what I prefer for breakfast. I close the distance between us, sliding my hands up her bare thighs. Her eyes question me as her lips form a perfect little 'O'. Hooking my thumbs into the waistband, I quickly slide her panties toward her knees, my eyes locked on hers. While hers ping-pong between mine, I remain focused. My eyes implore hers to see my need, my want, my absolute addiction to her. My palms slowly urge her knees to part. Her hazel eyes search mine for... for I don't know what. In answer, I fall to my knees, my face eye-level between her open thighs, in awe of the gift before me.

"Steph..."

My mouth connects with the apex of her thighs, the center of her pleasure. When my tongue laps once, twice upon her sensitive bud, her head falls back, thumping against the cabinet door. At war, my mind wants me to comfort the bump while my libido urges me to continue my ministrations until she screams my name. I focus on my task, the pleasure I desire to give to her, and the end game.

"Mmm," she moans, fingers splayed wide upon her thighs.

I alternate licking, sucking, and strumming, fueled by her whimpers, moans, and hitching breath. Her fingers find their way into my hair and at the back of my head, urging me not to stop. Instead of patting myself on the back, I double my efforts to deliver her ecstasy.

"Mm-hmm," she murmurs. "Right there. Oh. God. Yes."

My index finger caresses her inner walls as my thumb presses repetitive circles upon her clit.

"Fuck...Fuck...F-U-C-K!!!!" Sylvie pants loudly.

I press my mouth to her, my lips sucking her nub, elongating her orgasm. My free hand fumbles with my boxers as her inner walls contract over and over, grasping my fingers tight.

I rapidly withdraw my fingers and mouth, thank God I no longer need a condom, and slide inside, impaling myself deep within her heat.

Still contracting... the pressure... the heat... I let go. Her hands grab my ass, her fingernails biting my flesh as she milks every ounce of me, taking everything I have to give. My nerve endings from my ass cheeks send the alert of pain to my brain. My eyes closed, I draw in a long breath, registering the slight bite of pain her fingernails cut into my skin. Sensual. Delicious. Hot. I shudder, my legs shake, and my hands fall to the counter to prevent my fall. I press my forehead to hers, forcing my heavy eyelids to open.

I find her sated eyes peering back at me. The release is not enough; she leaves me wanting more. I heft her over my right shoulder. Her legs kicking in protest in front of me, I stride to her bedroom.

## Chapter Sixty-Six
# SYLVIE

"Stephen! Put. Me. Down!" I yell, my body hefted over his shoulder.

"You want down?" he rebuts. "Now you are down," he states as my body bounces on my bed.

I blink, and he's over me, pressed to me, his heat and weight upon me. He nips, he sucks, he kisses, and he bites.

I close my eyes but a minute, and he's in me and over me; he's everything to me. With every breath I pull in, I feel him. With every cell in my body, I feel him. He's everywhere, and I'm bathed in him.

My back arches, and my heartbeat quickens. I need this; I need him.

"Syl..." his husky voice whispers. "I'm... cum with me."

He only needs to ask; I obey. One... Two... Three... I'm over the peak. I'm there. I'm at the pinnacle of ecstasy; I'm in heaven.

A guttural groan escapes his chest. He's feral, shuttering.

It's heady, this ability, this knowledge that I affect him so. It's as if I'm his kryptonite. I fly high outside myself with this feeling of power.

His mouth covers mine, consumes mine, consumes me. His tongue invades, and he owns me. My hands rove his back, his ribs, and find purchase upon his buttocks. I hold him to me as I seek to ground myself by anchoring to him.

Many moments pass as we fall back from the edge of heaven. Our labored breathing finds a slower pace, and our racing hearts their healthy rhythm.

"I need a shower and food," I state, smiling.

"If we share a shower," Stephen smirks, his thumb caressing my cheek, "we'll eat sooner."

Doubting his logic, I slip from my side of the bed, padding into the bathroom and feeling the heat of his gaze on my naked backside.

---

The warm water and soapy bubbles ignite rather than calm my sensitive skin and desire. I bite my lower lip when a sensual idea enters my mind. I steal the soapy loofa from his hand, replacing it on the hook. Both under the spray, I lazily slide my fingertips over his shoulders, his chest, then his ribs. I drop one hand behind me as the other entwines with his. Backing up, my free hand guiding me, I take a seat on the tiled corner bench, pulling him with me.

Through my wet lashes, I look up for his approval. I sweep my index finger from his navel, following the thin smattering of hair down his happy trail. His eyes turn liquid, and that's my cue.

I take his cock in my left hand, enjoying the heavy weight of him in my palm. My tongue darts over my lower lip, barely swiping his sensitive tip. I giggle when it twitches, his rock-hard cock reaching for me. I should prolong his torture, but I'm too turned on myself.

## Chapter Sixty-Seven
# STEPHEN

Every muscle in my body flexes as Sylvie's hazel eyes, through her dark, wet lashes, seek mine. Her hot tongue slowly licks only the tip of me. It takes all of my strength to refrain from sinking myself into her mouth over and over again.

Sensing my need, she doesn't toy with me; her right hand grasps my hard shaft tightly, and her lips slide over me an inch at a time. I want to keep my eyes on her; I want to watch her mouth take me and her cheeks hollow out, but my eyes close as her warm, slick tongue and powerful lips work me. My left hand caresses the side of her head while my right palm on the tile wall holds me in place.

She sets an aggressive pace, sucking me in and out, her fist pumping in time. Though I've had her twice this morning, it's clear I won't last long under her ministrations. Her free hand clutches my ass, pulling me towards her on her downward strokes. It's my undoing.

"Syl," I moan, my voice husky. "Syl, I'm going to..."

In the blink of an eye, both her hands dig into my ass, holding me to her as she takes me deeper. So deep, I can feel the back of her throat. Lightning shoots down my spine, my thighs tense, and my orgasm explodes. Not wanting to hurt her, I attempt to pull out, but she refuses to release her tight grip on my backside.

Slowly my heavy eyes open to find hers staring up at me, a proud smile on her face. I slide the pad of my thumb over her swollen lower lip, and she rises to stand in front of me under the spray. I pull her to me, her head to my chest. I feel my hands tremble as they press into her back. Every part of me buzzes. She affects me in a way no woman has before.

Syl slips from the shower, allowing me to clean myself up. I turn the knob, silencing the spray, wrap a towel around my waist, and step from the shower to find Sylvie in my t-shirt, sitting on the vanity.

She doesn't hide her head-to-toe inspection of me. She bites her lip, liking what she sees.

"I think every day should be 'towel day'," I state, enjoying her ogling me.

"'Towel day' will need to wait until after you feed me," she counters, her head tilting to the side.

I grab my phone from the vanity, tap a few buttons, then replace it. "Done," I inform her, tilting my head as she did.

"What's done?" she queries.

"I ordered pizza," I state. "It will be here in 45 minutes."

She nods approvingly.

"Now back to 'towel day'," I growl, leaning into her. I press a kiss upon her lips before quickly throwing her over my shoulder and packing her back into the bedroom.

"Stephen!" she laughs, her legs flailing.

"Shush, woman," I tease.

She swats my backside, causing my towel to fall to the floor. When she gasps, I pause.

"Did I..." she whispers.

I bend, standing her on the floor at the end of the bed, my eyes questioning.

"I'm sorry. I didn't mean to hurt you," she murmurs.

It takes a moment, but I figure out she's talking about the red marks her nails caused on my ass.

I gently pinch her chin between my thumb and forefinger, holding her eyes to mine. "They don't hurt, and at the time, the sensation..." I struggle to explain. "It was hot."

She shakes her head, unbelieving.

"You didn't break skin." I tell her what she knows. "They'll disappear in a couple of hours," I promise.

I urge her eyes back to mine.

"It will be even hotter when I give you so much pleasure that you leave scratches up and down my back." I smile. "It'll be like the Buckcherry song you like and hot as hell."

"I can't believe you want me to hurt you," she murmurs, shaking her head.

"It's not painful during sex. It actually heightens the pleasure," I inform.

I slide my hand up under the tee, softly caressing her breast. I slip my other hand under as well, raising the shirt up, allowing my mouth to find her nipple. I gently suck before pulling away.

"It's like this," I state, my mouth returning to her breast. This time, my teeth gently tug at her nipple. When I pull away, my thumb continues to circle the puckered nub.

I look into her eyes, hoping she now understands that her fingernails don't hurt me; they're part of the entire sensual experience.

"I see," she whispers.

## Chapter Sixty-Eight
# STEPHEN

"Yo, you're doing it again," Fredrik chuckles from the driver's seat as we sit outside the funeral home.

Of course, I'm doing it. Sylvie's not someone you can forget.

"Like your mind is on the job right now," I motion towards the hearse parked beside us. "I'm sure you're thinking of Elizabeth and the kids. I mean, they're the reason we're working overtime today."

I don't mean this in a bad way. We're working funeral duty on our day off; it's not as if we're in any danger. I'll focus when I stand in the middle of the intersection to stop traffic for the funeral procession. Until then I prefer thinking of Sylvie to thoughts of death.

"You going over there after this?" he asks.

"Didn't make any plans yet," I mumble.

"Text her," Fredrik encourages.

"Huh?" I turn to face him.

"It's clear you can't keep her off your mind," he states the obvious. "Text her, make plans," he chuckles. "Elizabeth's worried you'll screw this up. I wouldn't be surprised if she doesn't talk to you daily to keep you from letting Sylvie slip away."

I shake my head. Elizabeth's already spoken to me about how much she likes Sylvie and that she's available for any advice I might need.

---

**Stephen: I'm fixing you dinner tonight**
**Me: OK**
**Stephen: be there @7**
**Me: Ok**

My insides flutter with excitement. I wonder what he'll prepare. I try not to get my hopes up; he could simply mean he's getting takeout. I hope he actually cooks. A vision of Stephen standing at my stove, causes me to smile. Seven hours--this will be a long afternoon.

---

"Pour yourself a glass of wine," Stephen instructs. "Then come to the patio and keep me company."

I quickly grab a beer for each of us, following him out back.

"One for you and one for me," I say, placing his beer on

the patio table with his ingredients. "What are you fixin'?"

While lighting the grill he shares, "New York strips, cream cheese stuffed Anaheim peppers wrapped in bacon and baked potatoes."

He smiles over his shoulder at me. "I hope you're hungry."

"Starving," I reply. "I forgot to eat lunch today."

"I thought you set an alarm to remind you to take a break. He turns to face me, tongs in his hand.

"I did. I took the dogs out, then started painting again without eating." I shrug. "I get enthralled in my work."

"How do you like your steak?" he asks, as he turns the foil-wrapped peppers and potatoes over.

"Well-done," I answer.

"Well, you'll try it medium tonight. Trust me, you'll love it." He clicks the tongs open and closed in my direction. I open my mouth to argue, but he continues, "No blood, I promise?"

I enjoy my beer as he grills, seasons, and turns the food. All the while, my stomach growls for the food he prepares, and my body yearns to gobble him up. I laugh at my thoughts; the new Sylvie always wants more.

"What's so funny?" he asks, beer near his lips.

I shake my head. "I'm drooling." *For him more than the steak*, I admit to myself, while biting my lip.

Stephen's thumb tugs my lip, startling me. *How'd I not hear him approach?* All thoughts cease as his warm mouth molds to feast on mine. Too soon, he pulls away.

"Steaks are done," he states and smirks.

My brow furrows and eyes squint as my foggy mind processes his words.

*Chapter Sixty-Nine*
# SYLVIE

Just off the phone with Lidia, I text Stephen before he starts his night shift on duty.

**Me: Cancelling my oral surgery tomorrow**
**Me: Lidia's ill & can't drive myself**

When a few moments pass, I figure I've missed him before he entered the station.

**Stephen: Don't cancel. I can drive you**
**Me: You'll be tired from work**
**Stephen: I rarely head straight to bed**
**Stephen: Let me drive you**

**Stephen: I can nap while I stay with you**
**Stephen: Until the anesthesia wears off**
**Me: I couldn't ask**
**Stephen: You didn't, I offered**
**Stephen: Let me do this for you**
**Me: Appt. at 9 takes 45 min**
**Stephen: I'll come straight from work**
**Stephen: About 8**
**Me: Thank you (heart emoji)**
**Stephen: Good night (kissing face emoji)**

---

## Stephen

After receiving a printout of Sylvie's post-operative instructions, the nurse helps her into the passenger seat of my truck. With her door shut and seat belt on, we head to her house.

"How are you feeling?" I ask, eyes on her while idling at a red light.

"Good," she says. "I should send a picture to Lidia."

She pulls out her phone, leans towards me, holds the camera to the side, and smiles for a selfie with me.

"Lidia's gonna love this one," she states as she types and sends the photo of the two of us.

"So, no pain?" I ask. I was told she'd be groggy and in pain.

"Nope," she replies, popping her 'P'. "What should we have for lunch?"

"Well, lunch is hours away. We're stopping for your prescriptions, then I'm taking you home to tuck you into bed." When I glance in her direction, she seems herself with no sign of grogginess.

I pull in the drive-up pharmacy lane and request her scripts. I'm told they will be ready in ten minutes, so I park us in the grocery parking lot to wait.

"I'm gonna run in to grab some pudding and soft food for me," she suggests. "It'll just take a minute, and I'll grab my scripts on the way out."

*Odd.* I squint my eyes, assessing her. She's not having trouble talking and she's able to send Snapchats, so she should be able to shop. I nod.

She climbs from the cab of my truck, purse in hand, without any trouble.

I people-watch while I wait for her to emerge from the store. Several long minutes pass, then she steps through the automatic doors, carrying several grocery bags.

I pull the truck up beside her, and she places all of the bags on the floorboard with her purse before climbing into the seat, a large smile on her face.

"I thought you were getting pudding and something soft. It looks like you bought way more than that," I tease. "Did you remember your prescriptions?"

She proudly lifts the paper pharmacy bag from the plastic ones on the floor.

---

I assist Sylvie from the truck and carry her shopping bags into the kitchen for her.

"Go change into comfy clothes, and I'll get the sofa ready for you to lay down," I order.

"For us to lay down," she corrects.

I pull a bag of white chocolate Reese's from one shopping bag then another. With all bags empty, I stare at the food covering her countertop. There are several bags of white and milk chocolate Reese's candy bars, a roll of chocolate chip cookie dough, two types of pudding cups, varieties of Chex cereal, and a large can of mixed nuts.

"Just leave them on the counter," she instructs. "That way, it will be easy for me to grab some," she says as she grabs a water and plops on the sofa.

I read through the post-op instructions again, marveling that she's not showing the symptoms I read about. I search her kitchen cabinets until I find some pain reliever. I pour two into my palm, then walk toward my patient.

"Thank you," she says, quickly downing the pills.

"I'm going to take the dogs out back for a bit," I inform as she positions herself on the pillow with a throw blanket.

I'm only outside 10 to15 minutes, but when I return, she's asleep. I position myself on the other end of the sectional sofa, encouraging the two dogs to lay with me and leave Sylvie alone. Unable to find something interesting on TV, I tilt my head back and close my eyes.

## Chapter Seventy
# SYLVIE

I open one eye then the other. My mouth hurts; I need some pain relievers. I slowly raise to a sitting position, freezing at the sight of Stephen asleep nearby with my puppy on his chest and Hagrid near his feet.

I snag my cell phone from the table in front of me and take two pictures; I have to record this moment. Of course, at my movement, the two dogs move, waking him up.

"Hey," he greets with sleepy eyes and a gruff voice. "How do you feel?"

"I hurt." I stand, and when he moves to join me, I order him, "Stay. I'm getting pain meds and laying back down."

He props his head on the back of the sofa, watching me move about the kitchen. I swallow two pills then take in all of the snacks on my kitchen island.

"What are these?" I ask, pointing to the counter.

"You went in the store for pudding and your prescriptions," he states. "Those are all the items you came out with."

I return to my end of the sectional. "I don't remember shopping," I admit, brow furrowed. Glancing down at my pajama shorts, I add, "I don't remember changing my clothes either."

Instantly, Stephen is alert. "You don't remember telling me you would go into the grocery store to get pudding and your meds?"

I slowly shake my head.

"You were talking and acting fine," he swears. "I wouldn't have let you go in by yourself if I'd thought you were out of it. You talked fine and took selfies on our way to the store."

I cringe. *Selfies? What did I take, and who did I send it to?* I open my phone, searching for photos. Then, I go to Snapchat. I see that I sent photos to Lidia, but I can't see what I sent.

"I don't remember leaving the oral surgeon," I grumble.

"Well, you are home and safe," he offers. "I should have known better than to let you shop."

I shrug, lay back down, and quickly fall back to sleep.

---

Stephen sleeps on my sofa. I feel bad that he worked all night then had to care for me this morning. I do my best to eat my pudding and take the dogs outside without disturbing him. I move a lounge chair under the patio umbrella and relax outside with the dogs.

*Why did I buy all of those candies while I went in for pudding?*

They aren't even treats I normally eat. I hope that all of the items were between the door and the dairy where I found pudding. I cringe at the thought of me seeming drunk, traipsing around the grocery store.

I'm outside an hour when Stephen joins me. "How do you feel?"

"I'm okay; pain relievers work if I take them without letting them wear all of the way off."

His hair is messed from sleep, and I smile.

"What's the cookie dough for?" I ask. "I found it when I grabbed a pudding cup."

He shakes his head, chuckling. "You bought it. When I tried to ask you why you bought all of those chocolates and cereals, you pointed your finger at me and said, 'Don't be judgy. I need soft, melt-in-my-mouth foods for a couple of days, so you can't be judgy.'" He bites his lips, attempting not to smile.

I shake my head, remembering none of it. "I'm afraid to ask," I chuckle. "I planned to make Chex Mix?"

He shrugs, a wide smile upon his exhausted face. "I guess I suck at taking care of patients."

We laugh.

"Wait!" I shout. "Did I pay for the groceries and prescriptions?"

"Everything was in a bag when you exited," he informs. "So, I assume you did."

"I better check," I state as I open my banking app on my phone. I breathe a huge sigh of relief when my account shows debits for today's purchases.

"Shouldn't you go back to sleep?" I ask.

"I'm off the next three days," he explains. "If I sleep now, I won't sleep tonight."

"Wow. That has to be a hard transition," I state.

"I'm used to it." He makes light of it.

## Chapter Seventy-One
# STEPHEN

**Sylvie: Still mtg @ Brickhouse?**
**Me: 6 sharp**

*I've worked double shifts. It seems like weeks since I've seen her instead of three days. We may meet at the bar, but I have other plans for the two of us tonight*, I think to myself. It's my nieces' birthday, and I plan to introduce Sylvie to the family. She seemed okay with meeting them at the Sunday barbecue that Mom cancelled when Dad had to go to urgent care for stitches a week ago.

My stomach flip-flops at the thought. I've never taken a woman to meet my family. I try to calm my nerves. We'll hang at the bar an hour or so. Then, we'll need to leave.

When I enter the smoky bar, it's a couple of minutes before six. Scanning the crowd, I can't see Sylvie anywhere. I slide onto a stool and order a beer at the bar. At the sound of a crackling mic, I turn towards the little stage. I freeze, beer in my hand, halfway to my open mouth.

"Hey. My name is Sylvie, and my therapist challenged me to take the stage. So, if I suck, it's all her fault." She shrugs. "But I'll have something to talk about in my next therapy session."

The crowd's laughter and applause fill the tiny bar. She strums her electric guitar once, and the crowd goes silent. A nervous smile upon her face, she nods to the audience in front of her, letting them know that she's ready. During this short silence, my heart beats loudly in my chest, and my throat grows dry.

She masterfully manipulates the six strings of her Fender guitar to play the National Anthem, reminiscent of a performance by Jimi Hendrix.

Taking a pull from my beer to wet my dry throat, I stare at her fingers prying each note out with their expert movements. Our previous conversation about her first time at the Brickhouse and checking out open mic night replays in my mind. At the time, I assumed she was pulling my leg. This little minx is full of surprises.

The bar is dark save for the stage lights focused on Sylvie's solo. She seems at ease, feet spread in a wide stance to allow her arms to move her fingertips over her instrument. Thoughts of my mother's CD collection spark to mind. Sylvie's short, blonde hair reminds me of Blondie from the 80's. Both are kick-ass rockers.

It's hard for me to imagine the version of Sylvie that

raised Lidia and married Omar. The Sylvie I know could never be muted; she's a force. I love this woman. I love her with every part of me. I love her to the point that I can no longer live without her.

The applause with whooping and hollering pulls me from my thoughts. Sylvie's cheeks turn red as the patrons refuse to end their celebration of her performance. Several sharp whistles join the voices and clapping.

She bows, her hands pressed together in front of her, then exits the stage. The lights over the bar brighten, allowing me to watch her place her guitar into its case.

Unable to remain seated, I stride in her direction. I forcefully push my way through the crowd that flows toward her. I fight down the growl rising in my chest, my need to assert my claim publicly bubbling up.

Sylvie leans her guitar case against the wall, turning toward the crowd.

My hands plant on her hips, I pull her tight to my chest, and my mouth takes hers. I ravage her for several long minutes, breaking our connection in need of oxygen. My forehead presses to hers, our mouths an inch apart, my eyes boring into her soul.

"Stephen," she whispers breathily. "People are staring."

"Let them stare," I growl.

Her hands slide to my chest, clutching the fabric of my shirt.

"Wanna get out of here?" she murmurs, a goofy smile upon her face.

## Chapter Seventy-Two
# SYLVIE

"Come inside. I'll only be a minute," I offer. "I just need to change from these smoky, bar clothes."

I enter the code, and the garage door rises. I hurry inside, not looking to see if Stephen follows. In my room, I step out of my jeans, leaving them on the floor. I wiggle my t-shirt over my head, stepping into my closet. My fingers glide from hanger to hanger, unsure what to wear to meet Stephen's family.

*I should have planned my attire earlier today.*

I slip into a pair of white shorts, a red halter top, and a pair of red flip-flops. Turning this way and that in front of the full-length mirror, I'm looking good and ready to go. Catching Stephen standing nearby, my skin sizzles under his approving gaze. I spin slowly to give him the full view.

"Okay to meet the family in this?" I inquire, placing my hands on his hips.

Stephen clears his throat. "It's perfect. And they are gonna love you. Don't worry."

"Ugh," I groan. "My hair smells like the bar; even I can smell it."

"We'll be outside. No one will notice," he promises. "Anyway, they all knew we were meeting for drinks tonight."

I tilt my head, smiling. "You told them?"

He nods.

"Let me see the picture of your nieces again," I beg, palm out between us.

Stephen quickly scrolls through his cell phone pictures then passes me his phone. I stare at the identical twins standing at his sides, the picture from earlier this summer.

"We can't show up without a gift," I state, heading for the stairs.

"I dropped the gift off earlier this week, so that's covered." He repeats what I already know.

"It's not in me to show up with no gift." As I descend the stairs, a plan forms in my mind. "I will only be a minute,"

Stephen follows me downstairs. He hasn't seen this part of my house before. In the storage area, I move a drop cloth and thumb through canvases standing long ways on a shelf. I pull out first one then a second painting. I slowly turn to show him.

I hold two canvases, each with a little blonde girl in a white sundress with yellow sunflowers, barefoot, on their knees in lush, green grass near a flowerbed. One painting has a butterfly in the little girl's palm. The other has an earthworm, and dark dirt speckles her hand.

## Chapter Seventy-Three
# STEPHEN

"Syl..." I shift my weight from one foot to the other, holding a painting in each hand. "Wow. That... Those are amazing and look exactly like the girls."

Sylvie turns them to face her, tilting her head to the side, scrutinizing her work. "May I see the picture of them again?"

Once more, I extend my phone.

"Hmm... I need to make one small addition. I'll be quick."

She darts up the stairs, both canvases in hand, and I do my best to follow. In her sunroom studio, she doesn't wear an apron but quickly and artfully adds brown undertones to the blonde hair in each painting.

"Now, it looks like the girls." She steps back proudly. While she blows a nearby hair dryer on each area for a couple of minutes, I have to admit that, with a few perfectly placed brush strokes, the paintings now look just like my nieces. I shake my head. She certainly has a finely tuned artist's eye.

I hold the paintings while she pulls two large brown paper bags and colored ribbons from the entry closet. She wraps white tissue paper around each canvas before sliding it into the large gift bag. Then, she creatively ties a large pink ribbon to one and a purple ribbon to the other. She writes 'Happy birthday!' on blank cards, slides each into a white envelope, then writes each name on one before securing it to the ribbons on each bag.

"I'm ready to go," she declares.

## Chapter Seventy-Four
# SYLVIE

Pulling up to his parents' house, I see several cars and trucks in the long driveway and parked on the street. Stephen carries the two bags in one hand, and his other splays across the exposed skin at the small of my back, guiding me around the side of the house to the backyard where I spot piles of gifts and helium balloons decorating a long table.

Patio chairs surround tables filled with adults as teens and younger children play tag amongst the manicured landscaping and trees.

"They're here! They're here!" Two little girls, in matching green sundresses, sprint toward Stephen and me, yelling and flailing their arms. They freeze in front of us. "Mom said we could open gifts when you got here."

"Are those for us?" One niece points to the large bags in Stephen's hand.

He nods. "Sylvie, this is Hanna and Madeleine," he introduces, pointing to each twin. "Carry these to the gift table, please."

They instantly do what their uncle asks, looking at the names on the cards, exchanging bags, then hurrying to the table.

"Momma?" they call while making their way to the table. "We can open now; Uncle Stephen is here."

"Only one before we eat." Stephen's older sister, Hillary, waves excitedly in our direction.

"I wanna open this one," they state in unison, and I freeze.

"You'll get used to it," Stephens whispers near my ear.

I turn, unsure what he means.

"They talk together and have their own twin language," he smiles. "You'll learn to ignore it."

"Let Uncle Stephen and Sylvie find a seat before you open that," she yells to her daughters.

"Hurry, Uncle Stephen," one girl urges.

"Yes, hurry and sit down," the other girl orders.

He pulls out an empty patio chair for me, then plants himself in one beside me.

"Okay. One... Two... Three..." Stephen yells, and the girls untie the bow and reach for the large gift inside.

"Freeze!" their mom orders, and they obey. "Who's it from?"

"It's from them." They point at us.

"Nope," his sister states.

The girls shrug at each other and reach for the card.

"Read it out loud," their mom orders.

"It's from her." Both girls stare wide-eyed at me.

"Happy birthday," I cheer, wishing the attention back on the girls and off of me. Soon, they tear into the tissue paper.

"Oh..." they gasp.

"I love it. I love it. I love it!" Hanna spins in a circle, admiring the art, her arms fully extended. "I love butterflies," she states, stopping in front of me. "Uncle Stephen, did you tell her I love butterflies?"

He shakes his head.

"Then, how did you know?" Madeleine asks.

I simply shrug, no idea how I luckily labeled the gifts for the twins.

"Thank you," the other twin says on her way to the man standing by her mom.

Stephen's sister's voice raises an octave. "Sylvie, you painted these?" It's both a question and a statement.

I smile back at her.

"I showed her the girls' photo on my phone," Stephen explains. "Next thing I know, she pulls out two paintings." He catches his breath. "I thought they looked just like the girls, but she said she needed to fix something. She made a few colored strokes through their hair, and here they are. Perfect."

His sister scrutinizes his boasting and admiration before smiling in my direction. Apparently, she enjoys seeing Stephen like this.

"Sylvie are you a painter?" one twin asks.

"She's an artist," the other twin corrects.

I nod.

"Can you teach me how to paint?"

"Me, too? Me, too?"

Stephen answers for me. "On my next weekend off, we'll all go to Sylvie's house to paint."

His nieces cheer.

"Time to eat," an older gentleman calls.

"That's my dad, Gordon," Stephen states, pointing toward the grill where his dad waves. "Mom is at the food table." Again, he points. "Mom, turn around and say hi to Sylvie."

I wave to his mother then the rest of the family as he introduces me to them.

"Stephen, why don't you go help Dad set out the food?" his sister directs. "I'll keep Sylvie company."

I smile to let him know I'll be okay.

She wastes no time, getting right to the point. "I like seeing Stephen so happy. You're good for him."

"I don't know about that. We have a lot of fun together," I respond.

"Like I said, you make him happy." She squeezes me with one arm around my shoulders, then guides me through the patio doors to the large family inside.

# EPILOGUE

**Stephen**

We found each other. In this crazy world somehow, we bumped into each other. Over and over, we bumped into each other. Fate, destiny, a higher power, or even blind luck, whatever it was that brought us together, I will be forever grateful.

We're not a traditional couple; that doesn't matter to us. We work. We fit. Others won't understand, for them our fourteen-year age difference is a non-starter. I have an old soul; she has a young heart. We work. They'll label her a cougar or Mrs. Robinson. Let them. We work. She's not a cougar she's my little minx.

It takes a strong woman to commit to a first responder. Not everyone can deal with the constant unknown, the danger, and the fear.

Sylvie is a pillar of strength. She assures me she can handle all that comes with my being an officer, and I'm starting to believe her. I feel myself letting her in, getting closer with each passing week. She's melding with my partner and my family. Our lives interlace; she's mine, and I'm hers. I was smart for keeping everything casual for years; it allowed me to be free when Sylvie slid into view. Little did I know, a noise complaint call on a warm, late-June night would forever change my life for the better.

# TRIVIA

1. The first and last names of *ALL* characters in this book are the names of world leaders. (Except Hagrid & Bocephus the dog.) Condoleezza Rice, Christina Fernandez de Kirchner, Edith Cresson, Elizabeth Queen, Hanna Suchocka, Helen Clark, Madeleine Albright, Michelle Bachelet, Sylvie Kinigi, Daniel Ortega, Felipe Calderon, Fredrik Reinfeldt, Gordon Brown, Hugo Chavez, Nelson Mandela, Omar Bongo, Stephen Harper, Winston Churchill
2. The character Dawn is based on my best friend. During a car ride, I explained my next series of books and she suggested I have one random character that appears in each book. Thus, I named the character after her and awarded her Dawn's positive spirit. In 2015 she was diagnosed with stage IV colon cancer. They found it late and

it had spread throughout her body. She has chemotherapy every two weeks for the rest of her life. With all of this she's still a ray of sunshine and lifts others, like me, up. Her strength and selflessness inspire me to try and improve myself. She's the most upbeat and positive woman I know. I absolutely love her laugh.

3. What are the seven deadly sins? The 7 deadly sins, also called 7 cardinal sins, are transgressions that are fatal to spiritual progress within Christian teachings. They include envy, gluttony, greed, anger or wrath, sloth, and pride. They are the converse of the 7 heavenly virtues.

4. Haley Rhoades is my penname. I created it using the maiden names 2 of my great-great-grandmothers on my father's side of our family.

# NEWS

Keep up on the latest news and new releases from Haley Rhoades.
**Text: Frogs to 444999**

Please consider leaving a quick review on Amazon, Goodreads, & Bookbub.

# ABOUT THE AUTHOR

Haley Rhoades's writing is another bucket-list item coming to fruition, just like meeting Stephen Tyler and skydiving. As she continues to write romance and young adult books, she plans to complete her remaining bucket-list items, including ghost-hunting, storm-chasing, and bungee jumping. She is a Netflix-binging, Converse-wearing, avidly-reading, traveling geek.

A team player, Haley thrived as her spouse's career moved the family of four eight times to three states. One move occurred eleven days after a C-section. Now with two adult sons, Haley copes with her newly emptied nest by writing and spoiling Nala, her Pomsky. A fly on the wall might laugh as she talks aloud to her fur-baby all day long.

Haley's under five-foot, fun-size stature houses a full-size attitude. Her uber-competitiveness in all things entertains, frustrates, and challenges family and friends. Not one to shy away from a dare, she faces the consequences of a lost bet no matter the humiliation. Her fierce loyalty extends from family, to friends, to sports teams.

Haley's guilty pleasures are Lifetime and Hallmark movies. Her other loves include all things peanut butter, *Star Wars*, mathematics, and travel. Past day jobs vary tremendously from an elementary special-education para-professional, to a YMCA sports director, to a retail store accounting department, and finally a high school mathematics teacher.

Haley resides with her husband and fur-baby in the Kansas City area. This Missouri-born girl enjoys the diversity the Midwest offers.

Reach out on Facebook, Twitter, Instagram, or her website...she would love to connect with her readers.

- amazon.com/author/haleyrhoades
- facebook.com/AuthorHaleyRhoades
- twitter.com/HaleyRhoadesBks
- instagram.com/haleyrhoadesauthor
- goodreads.com/HaleyRhoadesAuthor
- bookbub.com/authors/haley-rhoades
- pinterest.com/haleyrhoadesaut

Made in the USA
Middletown, DE
06 May 2022

65265910R10146